MW00640237

Security Breach

Cyber Division Series
Complete Set

Security Breach

Cyber Division Series
Complete Set

Book 1: Fading into the Night

Book 2: Midnight Strike

Book 3: Daybreak

Book 4: High Noon

By Vannetta Chapman

SECURITY BREACH Cyber Division Series Complete Set
Copyright © 2020 by Vannetta Chapman

FADING INTO THE NIGHT © 2019 by Vannetta Chapman
MIDNIGHT STRIKE © 2019 by Vannetta Chapman
DAYBREAK © 2020 by Vannetta Chapman
HIGH NOON © 2020 by Vannetta Chapman

This title is available as an e-book.
Visit www.vannettachapman.com.

ALL RIGHTS RESERVED. No part of this publication may be reproduced,
stored in a retrieval system, or transmitted in any form or by any means—
electronic, mechanical, photocopy, recording, or any other—except for brief
quotations in printed reviews, without the prior permission of the publisher.

Requests for information should be addressed to:
VannettaChapman (at) gmail (dot) com

Any Internet addresses (websites, blogs, etc.) and telephone numbers in this
book are offered as a resource. They are not intended in any way to be or im-
ply an endorsement by the author, nor does the author vouch for the content
of these sites and numbers for the life of this book.

Note: This novel is a work of fiction. Names, places, and incidents are either
products of the author's imagination or used fictitiously. All characters are
fictional, and any similarity to persons living or dead is purely coincidental.

Cover design: Tranquility Press; Interior design: Henscratches.com

First printing, 2020
ISBN: 978-1-7340460-1-4 (print)
ASIN: B087V7P5C7 (ebook)

Contents

Fading into the Night

Cyber Division, Book 1

Dedicated to
My Readers

While this novella is set against the real backdrop of Shipshewana, the characters as well as the community are fictional. There is no intended resemblance between the characters in this book and any real members of the Amish community. As with any work of fiction, I've taken license in some areas of research as a means of creating the necessary circumstances for my characters. My research was thorough; however, it would be impossible to be completely accurate in details and descriptions, since each and every community differs. Therefore, any inaccuracies in the Amish lifestyles portrayed in this book are completely due to fictional license.

Contents

"Grow in the grace and knowledge of
our Lord and Savior Jesus Christ."
~2 Peter 1:5-8

"Technology is, of course, a double edged sword.
Fire can cook our food but also burn us."
~Jason Silva

᪣

Prologue

Nora Brooks stared at her boss across his desk. She'd been called in to the Virginia office for a briefing. She'd guessed it was about Dash, a cyber terrorist she'd personally been chasing for much too long. She knew that he was active again, knew something was about to hit, but she had no idea it would be this big.

"So we know where he is."

"We don't. We know where he was."

She waved away his reservations. "Send me. I'll find him."

"Nora, I want you to listen to me."

Jason Anderson was fifty-two years old, with gray short-cropped hair, a don't-waste-my-time demeanor, and a scar that ran from the outside of his left eye to his jaw. He'd never told her how the injury occurred, but she'd heard the rumors. They only caused her to respect him more.

He pinched the skin at the base of his throat and gestured toward the chair. When she'd sat—on the edge because she didn't plan on being there long—he steepled his fingers and cleared his throat.

"The perpetrator you call Dash..."

"It's his signature."

"He's contacted over twenty small municipalities."

"How small?"

"Ranging from under five hundred to a couple thousand."

"And he's demanding the same ransom amount as before?"

"He is." Jason waited for her to put it together.

"They don't have cyber insurance, and they won't have the funds to pay the ransom."

"Exactly."

"So what does he want?"

"He wants to force our hand. Our best guess? He's behind the bill for the government to provide cyber insurance to every municipality in America."

"You think Dash is the driving force for pending federal legislation?"

"Nearly two hundred companies are now providing cyber insurance domestically. He could be working for any one or even a combination of them."

"And their motive—"

"Is money. It's always money. US cyber premiums have topped $2 billion. If this legislation goes through, that amount will be a drop in the bucket."

Nora heard a pounding in her ears as her heart rate accelerated. If she'd caught him last time, they wouldn't be dealing with this now. She didn't blame herself. The man was slippery as an eel, but she had vowed that she would stop him before he managed to strike again.

"What is he threatening to do?"

"The usual—compromise the water supply,

bring down the grid, and get this..." He pulled a sheet of paper out from the stack on his desk and repositioned his glasses. "Pay the ransom or chaos will explode in little towns across America."

"He has a bomb?"

"It's possible."

"What options do we have?"

"As you pointed out, the small towns can't afford the ransom, and they don't have cyber insurance. The federal government could step in and pay it, but..."

"But we won't, because we don't negotiate with terrorists."

"You and I both know that we do negotiate with terrorists if it's expedient to do so. Our analysts say it wouldn't make any difference in this situation. Dash is making a point. If we cave now, he'll be back next week or next month demanding twice as much."

Nora sat forward, elbows on her knees, and rubbed her fingertips up and down her jaws. Finally she straightened up, having made her decision. Now all she needed was her boss's permission.

"I assume you called me in here because you've found a digital footprint."

He motioned her over to the U.S. map on the wall, and tapped a pin on the NE corner of Indiana. "Here. A little town called Shipshewana."

"Never heard of it."

"It's small. Six hundred residents."

"I don't get it. He'll stand out like a Great Dane in a litter of miniature poodles."

"There's a catch." He crossed his arms, feet planted firmly and eyes drilling into hers. "The place is a tourist destination."

"What do people go there to see?"

"The Amish."

"What's that?"

"Not what, who. Surely you've heard of Amish people."

"Not really."

"They're plain—conservative. They dress old-fashioned, live old-fashioned."

"So why would a cyber terrorist hide among a group of conservatives?" She snapped her fingers. "They're the people without electricity."

"Exactly. No electricity, no security cameras, no real way to track someone. If you think about it, he picked the perfect spot."

"Certainly everyone in..." she leaned toward the map, squinted, and said slowly, "Ship she wana..."

"Shipshewana."

"Whatever. Everyone there can't be Amish."

"No, it's about fifty-fifty, though even the locals try to emphasize the plain life. It's what tourists go there to see. Allowing folks to glimpse the Amish lifestyle has provided jobs and prosperity for the area—for everyone in the area."

"Okay. You're assigning me to Shipshewana, right?"

"If you want it."

"I do." She didn't hesitate, didn't have to think about it. If Dash was in a town of 600, she'd find him. "I'll send you hourly updates. Tate Woods has been activated already and will meet you at the airstrip. I'll forward details of the assignment to your phone."

"Thank you, sir."

"Nora," He waited for her to make eye contact.

"Be careful."

Nora nodded once and glanced at the map as she left the office. Twenty pins had been stuck into twenty locations that represented twenty towns in danger. Theirs was a small task force. Dash knew what he was doing. He was spreading them thin. They could ask for more personnel, but that request would be leaked, and it would make his point for him. Cyber terrorism was a real threat, and insurance was the only way to prepare for it—or so he wanted everyone to believe.

Well, she for one was not going to be a victim. She also wasn't going to be held hostage by a cyber punk. She would go to Indiana, find Dash, arrest him if he was cooperative and kill him if he wasn't.

In other words, she'd do her job.

ço

Benjamin Lapp didn't mind living on the farm alone, or at least that's what he told himself.

Sitting down at the large table to eat alone— that was a different matter. During those moments, instead of feeling satisfied with a good day's work, instead of appreciating the view of his farm outside the window... the memories wash over him.

Four brothers and three sisters, all crowded around the table.

His *mamm*, wiping the sweat from her forehead as she pulled dinner out of the oven.

His *dat*, walking in through the mudroom, stomping his boots, and delivering his favorite line. "What's the occasion, that we are having this bountiful meal?"

It was no occasion. It was simply their life, and it was good.

So much had changed since then. Life was still good, but it was different and Ben felt stuck. He didn't really know how to move forward, so instead he did the things he was supposed to do—raised crops in the Indiana dirt, cared for the buggy horse and the old cow, ate and slept and worshipped and rose at sunrise each day to do it all over again.

Crickets chirped outside the open window.

A slight breeze stirred the leaves of the old maple tree.

Molly, his single dairy cow, mooed from the barn. How was it that he was able to hear that? Or perhaps he only imagined he heard it. Molly was always eager for her evening milking. If there was one constant in his life, it was the habits and needs of that cow.

He stared down at the dinner on his plate—if you wanted to call it that. Cold ham, sliced tomatoes and cucumbers from the garden, and okra he'd half-heartedly attempted to stew in a pan. He really needed a cooking class or a wife.

That thought should have made him laugh, but it didn't.

"You're becoming morose," he muttered to himself. Then he stabbed the ham and forced himself to eat the dinner. It was while he was washing the single dish, knife, and fork, that he heard something.

Something unusual. Something that didn't belong.

He must be imagining things, because he thought he'd heard the click of a handgun. Personally he only owned a rifle and a crossbow, but the sound was close enough to the same.

He dried his hands on a dishtowel, placed the towel back on the hook, then moved to the window.

The sun had set while he was doing the dishes. The yard, barn, and fields looked as they should. And then he heard the footstep—shoe on gravel.

The person was walking slowly, carefully. Why would that be?

He glanced into the living room at the rifle which rested in a mount on the wall.

Nein. He wouldn't be needing that. More than likely what he'd heard had been some *youngies* messing around, perhaps they were trying to take something. Amish youth were good kids in general, but even they made bad decisions. Perhaps someone needed money for a phone bill. He'd just have to go out there and set them straight.

He left the rifle, opened the door as quietly as possible, and stepped out into the night.

Instead of striding out into the open, he waited.

There it was again, the same careful footstep on gravel—heel to toe, but this time near the barn.

He made his way around on the south side where the ground was covered with grass, where he wouldn't be heard. No use announcing his presence until he knew who and what he was dealing with.

He had the absurd thought that it might be a mountain lion. There had been reported sightings in the last few years, though none of them confirmed. Perhaps he should have fetched the rifle, but he could have never brought himself to shoot such an animal. Still, perhaps a shovel or rake—anything to wave and scare it off would have been a good idea.

Too late for that.

He was already creeping toward the back corner of the barn.

Ben Lapp thought he understood what life had in store for him. He thought there were no surprises left and certainly that there was no danger to be found on his little acreage. But life had always been full of surprises, of things that he didn't and couldn't understand. This was one of those moments.

Chapter 1

Benjamin Lapp walked around the corner of his barn and found himself staring down the barrel of a handgun. He froze mid-step. The woman holding the gun had her finger on the trigger.

"Easy." He said the one word in what he hoped was a low, calming voice.

"Hands up." "*Ya*. Okay."

"Turn around. Walk to the barn."

The sun had already set over her shoulder, and night had nearly fallen. But there was a sliver of light remaining, enough to see the sweat beading on her forehead, her labored breath beneath the black vest, and the blood running down her right arm.

He walked slowly. No need to spook her more than she already was.

The sound of that first shot had sent him out into the night to see what had happened. He didn't doubt that the second would stop his heart.

When they'd stepped into the coolness of the barn, she motioned him toward the workbench. "Sit."

Moving to the window, she divided her attention

between the gathering darkness and him.

Ben didn't speak. He did slowly lower his arms, but she immediately raised the gun.

"Keep them up."

He'd never argued with a woman holding a gun, and he didn't plan to start now.

Then again, the only woman he'd ever known to hold and shoot a firearm—a rifle not a handgun— had been his mother, and he wouldn't have messed with her if she were holding a mop.

Stepping away from the window, the woman pressed her back to the wall. "You don't talk much."

"*Nein*. I'm not exactly sure what to say in this situation."

"You've got the accent down. I'll hand you that."

"What accent?"

"And the clothes? What did you do, steal them off a clothesline?"

"Not too many six and a half foot Amish men hanging about. I assure you, the clothes are mine."

"Save it."

She continued to study him for several minutes. Finally she said, "Turn the lights on. Just one."

"I can't."

"Do not test me."

"Of course not. That is—I'd be happy to turn the lights on, but there aren't any."

"Aren't any what?"

"Lights."

"What are you talking about?"

"Amish farm—no electricity. There's a gas lantern...over there on the shelf."

She shook her head once, a curt definitive

motion. Did she think he'd try to burn the place down? Why would he do that to his own barn? And how would it help him in this situation?

"Flashlight?" she asked.

"*Ya*. Top shelf over by the office."

"You get it."

He moved slowly, carefully, retrieved the flashlight, switched it on, and placed it on the workbench facing toward the ceiling.

"Tell me what you're planning."

"I don't know what you're talking about."

"Is it a bomb?"

"A what?"

She stared at him another minute, her eyes piercing his with such hatred that Ben couldn't begin to imagine what the person she thought he was had done. Because one thing was certain—he'd never met her before. He would remember if he had. She was short—a full foot shorter than him—but what she lacked in height she made up for in intensity. Her hair was red and cut to frame her face. Her body—*compact* was the word that came to mind. There wasn't an ounce of extra on the woman, a fact made obvious by her tight-fitting black clothes. Definitely not Amish.

"If it were up to me, I would have put a bullet in your head when you walked around the side of the building."

"But you didn't."

"Because it's not up to me. Tell me the plan."

"I don't have a plan."

"Tell me where the bomb is. My boss has agreed to cut you a deal, against my protests."

"Because you would shoot me."

"Do not mock me."

In the soft light he could just make out the wound on her upper right bicep. Blood had soaked through the fabric of her shirt, rendering it glossy in the low light. Occasionally he thought he saw a tremor in her arm, which wasn't comforting in the least. She was holding the gun with her right hand.

"You're hurt."

She didn't respond, as if he hadn't even spoken.

"I have some medical supplies in the office. Accidents happen all the time in a barn. Let me get the kit for you."

"Is it on an automatic timer?"

"Is what on an automatic timer?"

"Did you hide it in the market?"

"What? *Nein*."

"Stop. Just stop lying."

"I'm not."

A low moan came from the back of the barn. She jerked the gun up and toward it.

"Hey. Take it easy."

She was already behind him, prodding him to his feet with her good arm, then pushing the flashlight into his hands and urging him forward. Could he overpower her? Doubtful. She'd shoot him before he could even turn around. She'd made that abundantly clear. Best to bide his time—hope and pray that she passed out from the wound. Then he could fetch a doctor and maybe find out what this was all about.

"Toward the back, slowly."

"It's Molly. She needs milking. It was what I was about to do when I heard something outside."

"What did you hear?"

"A shot—maybe. Didn't know it at the time, just heard the pop. No doubt the same shot that hit you in the arm." Which was when he realized that they weren't alone. Of course they weren't. Someone had shot the woman, and it hadn't been him.

They'd reached Molly's stall. The cow turned her head toward them—large brown eyes and a tuft of brown hair poking up between her velvety soft ears. She let out another baleful cry.

"I don't understand what's going on here, but I need to take care of Molly." Ben had his back to the woman. He didn't turn around, didn't raise his voice or make any quick moves. But he did proceed into the stall.

"Stop."

"She needs milking. Cows get used to a certain schedule."

"I said stop."

"And if you miss that schedule it's uncomfortable—painful even, as you can tell by the look she's giving me."

He continued forward, expecting at any moment to hear the click of the trigger, feel the searing pain of the bullet. He'd been struck by a bullet once before, when he was a child and hunting with his brother. They'd been messing around and the rifle had gone off. It was a pain he'd never forget and certainly didn't want to experience again. But then there was Molly...

He walked forward and righted the milking stool.

ço

Nora couldn't believe what she was seeing.

This guy was good. He had the clothes, the accent, even a name for the cow.

Which wasn't fooling her.

The tremor hit her arm again. She switched the gun to her left hand.

"That arm is only going to get worse unless you let me clean and bind it. I'm guessing you don't want to see a doctor."

He cleaned the cow's udders, slipped a pail underneath it, and proceeded to milk the beast.

The cow tossed him another look, as if to say *it took you long enough*, and commenced to eating more hay out of a wire basket attached to the stall's wall.

As Nora watched his strong hands expertly and quickly milk the cow, she realized she'd made a mistake. Whoever had shot her wasn't in this stall. Whoever had shot her, the same person who was planning an attack on Shipshewana, was still out there.

᭩

Chapter 2

She sat at the kitchen table, the Sig Sauer P226 on the table in front of her.

"Where did you learn to clean wounds?"

"Live on a farm long enough and you learn how to do most things that need to be done." He'd cut away the sleeve and cleaned both the entry and exit wound. "This is going to sting."

She made a motion for him to get on with it.

Whatever was in the brown bottle he was holding felt like a liquid knife. She clamped her teeth together until the spots in front of her eyes faded.

"Not sure what Mamm put in this exactly, but she always insisted it would kill any bacteria." He applied a pressure bandage and then wrapped the arm. "See if you can move it."

She raised her elbow, grimaced, and lowered it. "I'm good."

He'd put a glass coffee pot on the old gas stove as soon as they'd come in the house. Now he poured the hot brew into two mugs and brought them to the table along with milk, sugar, and a plate of oatmeal bars.

She hadn't eaten since her flight from DC that morning. She consumed one of the bars and downed half the coffee, which was bitter and acidic.

"My name is Ben...Ben Lapp, in case you were wondering."

She hesitated a moment, then said, "Nora...Nora Brooks."

"So what convinced you that I wasn't the guy you're looking for?"

She snorted and reached for another one of the bars. "Dash could not have milked a cow."

"How can you be sure?"

She drained the cup of coffee and ran her left hand up and down her jaw line.

Ben jumped up and refilled the cup.

"The profilers say he was raised in the urban jungle. Which urban jungle they haven't pinned down, but he's definitely a city kid."

"And he's here...in Indiana?"

"In Shipshewana. We know that too because we were able to patch together the data...he's good, bounces his signals off international servers, but any electronic communication can be traced if you're willing and able to dedicate the resources. And if you have the motivation to do so."

"So you followed his...signal."

"Which disappeared at your farm."

"Ah."

"What?"

"This area is a black hole as far as cell service, or so the Englisch say." Ben shrugged. "I wouldn't know."

Nora glanced around. She had the distinct impression that she'd stepped back in time—gas lanterns, no television, no computers or phones for that matter, no electricity at all. "It's the perfect place if you think about it."

"Here?"

"Yeah. There's no way to follow him. No CCTV."

"I don't know what that is."

"Closed-circuit television camera, which can be helpful when you're chasing a terrorist."

"I've never seen a camera on an Amish farm."

"And most of the businesses in town are too small to need one. No data signals. No electronic signature. It's like he just...faded into the night."

"After he shot you."

"Yeah. He got lucky. That won't happen again." "What does he want?"

"That's complicated, and I'm not authorized to tell you."

Ben nodded as if that made sense.

Nora walked to the sink, rinsed out the cup, then stared out the window considering her options. As far as she could tell there was no choice to make. If she was going to have any help from the locals—and in this situation she definitely needed help—her only option was sitting at the kitchen table, wearing black pants, a white shirt, and suspenders.

She'd made do with less.

And the clock was running on this. She glanced at her watch. Less than twenty-four hours. They needed to get to work.

ço

Ben still had no idea what was happening. The

woman was obviously with the military or some civilian authority. So why was she alone? Who was this Dash fellow? And why would he want to hurt people in Shipshe?

If there was one thing Ben had learned in his thirty-eight years of living on this Earth, of being Amish and seeking a simple life, it was patience. He didn't rush her. Didn't ask his questions. She'd tell him or she wouldn't, and it would be on her time. There was nothing vulnerable about Nora Brooks, but there was an intensity and purpose that was disarming. Try as he might, he couldn't hold it against her that an hour earlier she'd been pointing a gun at him.

He knew she'd made her decision when she turned from the window and sat down across from him.

"You've lived here a long time?" "All my life."

"Communications we've intercepted indicate that he might be hiding among your people."

"Among the Amish? I doubt that's possible." "You'd be surprised what he's capable of. Dash might not be able to milk a cow, certainly he wouldn't have the hands of a farmer in the short time he's been here..."

Ben looked down at his hands—scarred, tanned, working hands. His *dat* had always said you could tell a lot about a person by their hands. "So he's a computer guy."

"Yeah. Probably hasn't done manual labor an hour of his miserable life."

"If he's been here longer than a few days, he has. In an Amish community, everyone works."

"He's like a chameleon." She pressed the palm of her hand against the table in frustration. "We've been close before, and always he's faded into the surrounding population. Once it was a hippy colony in the northwest, another time executive yacht owners in Florida."

"And he planted bombs all those times?" Ben didn't make it a habit to follow the national news, but he was surprised he hadn't heard of either of these disasters.

"No. Before, he's stuck to taking out the power grid for a few hours. Once he threatened to contaminate a water supply—and we later found that everything was in place to actually accomplish it. We found it because he wanted us to find it. He wanted us to know what he was able and willing to do. This time he's taking his threats to a new level."

"I'll admit to being fairly naïve about technology, but why would he risk coming here? Can't he do what you described from his computer?"

"He can, but he seems to like the thrill of the chase. Our Dash is a real psycho. Or maybe he just wants our people to be here when it happens. Deal a blow to the agency while he's making good on his threats."

"So there are other people from your agency here?"

She rubbed her right eyebrow, then dropped her hands to her side. "Dash is part of a bigger network—a team of insurgents that are planning similar attacks on at least twenty different locations. We're spread pretty thin."

That explained her intensity, her desperate focus. For whatever reason, she was doing this alone. "When?"

Nora glanced at her watch. "Less than twenty-four hours."

"What does he want?"

Her right hand reached out and touched the weapon. "What do they always want? Money."

"Must be an easier way to get it."

"If we find him, you can tell him that."

"What can I do?"

She appraised him a moment, and he wondered what she saw. An Amish man, no longer young but not yet old. A working man, as she'd said, tall and lean and completely unfamiliar with the world she was describing.

"Do you have a weapon?"

"I have a rifle and a crossbow."

"Get the rifle."

He stood, walked into the living room, and returned with the T3x Hunter, bolt-action rifle. He'd bought it the year before because it reminded him of his grandfather's .308 Winchester. The stock was smooth, the sight true. He'd hunted deer with it the previous winter, turkeys in the spring. Since then, only wild hogs.

He handed it to her, and she held it in both hands, looked down the barrel, and pulled back the bolt.

"Capacity?"

"Three plus one."

"This is too obvious. You can't carry it down Main Street in the middle of the day. You're sure you don't have a handgun?"

"I think I'd remember if I did. Plus I'm Amish—our *Ordnung* forbids violence of any kind."

She raised an eyebrow, glanced down at the rifle in her hands, then handed it back to him with a skeptical look on her face. "That rifle runs a thousand bucks, at least."

"Twelve hundred."

"And probably another five hundred for the scope."

"It's for hunting. Many Amish are avid hunters. The meat is lean, no preservatives, and most of all, free. This rifle paid for itself the first year."

She stood and paced back and forth in front of the table. Finally she turned toward him, hands on her hips. "You're no good to me if you won't shoot that thing, if you won't defend yourself. Because Dash? He will kill you without a second thought."

Ben shrugged. "*Gotte* knows the number of my days."

"I have no idea what that means."

He didn't attempt to explain. He didn't know how, and he doubted she wanted an explanation of his faith. What she did want to know was whether she could trust him.

"You say this man...this Dash...has a bomb?"

"If the communication we intercepted is authentic, if it isn't a red herring to make us look the other way? Yeah, he has a bomb, and it's supposed to go off at seven o'clock tomorrow evening in downtown Shipshewana."

Ben stood, walked to the living room, and returned with the recent edition of their local paper. Dropping it on the table, he said, "Big concert tomorrow night—outdoors, near the Market."

"Do a lot of people attend?"

"*Ya*. Lots of people."

Ben walked past her, rinsed out his coffee mug, and stared out the window into the darkness. It had been seven months since his parents perished in a buggy accident. He thought he'd accepted it, but that deep well of grief still threatened to consume him at times.

He believed what he'd said.

They each had an appointed number of days, but that knowledge did little to relieve the loneliness of the life he was living. He'd wondered many times since his parents passed what his purpose was. Why wasn't he in the buggy too when the pick-up truck had crossed the line and ended their lives, the horse's life, in some ways Ben's life? Was it so important that he continue to farm the land, put in the crops, and milk Molly? What was his purpose in life?

And yet God had brought this *Englisch* woman to his doorstep, with her tale of danger and urgency. Perhaps, standing before him in the person of Nora Brooks, was his purpose. Stranger things had happened.

He turned around to face her, his backside against the kitchen cabinet, and his arms crossed.

"I'll help you. We'll find this Dash, but what happens after we find him is up to you. I can't...I couldn't take another life, no matter the reason."

"Are you good with this rifle?"

"Took a buck at three hundred yards."

"So maybe you could wound him...if it came to that."

Ben shook his head. "It doesn't work that way."

He glanced at the clock in the kitchen, the only clock in the house. The hands had just inched past ten p.m. If what she said was true, they had less than twenty-four hours to catch this Dash fellow and prevent the attack.

But Ben didn't know of any *Englischer*

masquerading as an Amish man.

Honestly, he only saw folks on Sundays, and he often hurried home as soon as it was polite to do so. His world had shrunk since his parents died. Perhaps that had been a mistake.

Atlee would still be up. He'd had trouble sleeping lately—mostly because of his arthritis, but Atlee insisted it was the spirit of God calling him to pray. He'd be awake.

"You said this Dash has been here, in Shipshe, and hiding among the Amish?"

"We think so, yes." "How long?"

"His signal disappeared two weeks ago. We caught a whiff of it early yesterday. I travelled here from D.C. on the first flight. Followed what we thought was his signal for a few hours, which is when you found me outside your barn. The trajectory of his electronic signature...it pointed this way."

"And someone shot you, right before I stepped outside?"

"I never saw him, so I suspect he was using a high powered scope from a fair distance." She worked her right arm up and down. "It can't be that hard to find one imposter in your midst."

"The Amish population here is quite large."

"Shipshewana has a population under five hundred. I checked."

"True, but most of the Amish farms are technically outside of town, so they wouldn't be in that number. We number twenty thousand in the state, and the largest group is here in the LaGrange/ Elkhart area. On market days? Lots of tourists. I've heard the number of folks in Shipshe alone swells to over thirty thousand."

"And a police force of half a dozen. No wonder he chose this spot." Nora stared across the room. "I need a plan. I can't sit here and wait for Dash to make the next move."

"How about we go and see my bishop?"

Chapter 3

While Ben hitched up the buggy, Nora walked the perimeter of the house and out buildings with a flashlight and retraced her steps. He found her outside the barn, crouched down and studying footprints in the dust.

"These are mine."

"And those are mine—I have big feet."

"He wasn't here that I can tell."

"Where were you standing when you were shot?"

She pointed to the far side of the barn. "I was closer to the house than the barn, and the shot came from...there." She pointed to the pump house, which was on a small rise to the west of the barn. They covered the ground quickly, then separated, both looking for any evidence that Dash had been in the vicinity. They met back at the front of the structure.

"Sun would have been at his back if he were standing here." Ben raised an imaginary rifle to his eye. "Pretty easy shot with the right equipment."

Nora pointed the flashlight at the ground. It took another five minutes before they found the heel print of a tennis shoe. "Not yours?" She asked.

"All I have is work boots—old ones and less old ones."

"Any kids around?"

"Not here. We're pretty far out from town. No reason they would have been here, and I would have noticed a group of *youngie*."

She splayed the flashlight around, finally zeroing in on a cigarette butt. "You don't smoke."

"Never have."

"All right. So he's standing here, for whatever reason, when he sees me arrive."

"How did you get here? I didn't see or hear a car."

"Plane, helicopter, feet."

"Ahhh."

"I'm following the signal, which led me here, and he's waiting at this spot, sees me enter the property, waits until he has a clear shot. But he would have had that at any time."

"He was waiting for the sun to settle against the horizon. Clear shot for him, and less chance you'd see him. Sounds like he planned a trap and you walked into it."

"Dash shot me when I wasn't quite to the barn. I thought I knew the direction the sound came from, so I came around the west side with my gun raised..."

"And nearly shot me." Ben raised his hands in surrender.

"No offense."

"None taken."

She shook her head. "Why was he out here? He couldn't just sit around hoping I'd show. There has to be another reason. What's past your property?"

"Nothing. More farms." He snapped his fingers. "But the church district line isn't far...just two places down."

"All right. So maybe he knows that we know he's infiltrated one of the local groups. He's walking a line between the two..."

"Which he only has to do for another..." Ben checked his watch. "Twenty hours."

"Right." She stood and dusted off her hands.

"Let's go see your bishop."

త

Nora had an irrational urge to get out of the buggy and jog...surely it would be faster.

Ben didn't seem at all disturbed by their pace— or lack of pace.

She felt as if she'd landed on another planet. She understood that she was completely out of her element, which was no doubt exactly what Dash had wanted. Sometime over the last year, this had become personal between them.

Nora's grandparents had been farmers, but she hadn't been to Texas since she was a young girl. The place had been sold long ago. She had fuzzy memories of petting goats and once riding on an old sway-backed horse. That was all so long ago, but deep down those memories were precious. They reminded her what she was fighting for. They reminded her that the people she protected were real people with farms and goats and sway-backed horses, with family and friends.

Perhaps her grandfather was why she'd recognized Ben for what he was—a farmer. Ben's hands looked like her grandfather's. She could still remember the feel of her small hand in his—how rough and large and comforting it had been. Those memories came from so long ago she felt like they belonged to a different person.

The last ten years had been training and missions and more training to try and keep up with the terrorists who were winning the race as far as technology. Always the agency was one step behind, and the cybercrimes were perpetrated faster than the agency could keep up.

The entire grid was vulnerable, but no one seemed to realize that. It was as if the general population wasn't able to process what the grid going down would mean. People didn't understand that water and traffic control and 9-1-1 calls all depended on electricity. The great majority of people only knew that things worked, and they expected things to continue to work.

Which was part of the reason the few cyber-attacks that had occurred had gone unreported. No one wanted to spook the public.

In Nora's opinion, people needed to be spooked. They needed to wake up.

Ben finally directed the horse down a dirt lane that ended at a sprawling one-story house. Instead of pulling up to it, he turned down a secondary lane and stopped in front of a small bungalow-type house. "Atlee's son lives in the big house with his children... ten last time I counted. Atlee lives in the *Dawdi Haus*."

The old guy must have been up and awake because he opened the front door before Ben had set the brake and hopped out of the buggy.

Twenty minutes later she shook her head in disbelief. She'd expected this to be difficult. The old guy wouldn't believe her, or he wouldn't understand the urgency of the situation. Maybe he'd have a touch of dementia. Possibly he'd be alarmed by what she said.

But Atlee did none of the things she'd expected. He listened, took her at her word, and when she was finished providing what few details she felt like she could share, he'd asked how he could help.

"We need to find Dash. It can't be that hard. He would have appeared within the last ten to fourteen days."

"Unless he laid the groundwork beforehand."
"What do you mean?"

"He could have been working on this plan for years." Atlee's hair was whiter than unpicked cotton. His beard reached to his shirt, and his skin was more wrinkled than a well-used map. But his eyes were clear and blue. "Maybe this man you're seeking pretended to have a relative that knew someone here. Happens all the time. Young man shows up on the bus, says he knows someone who knows someone. We have no reason not to trust him. Who would want to pretend to be Amish?"

Nora glanced at Ben who was nodding in agreement.

"All right, but even if he's visited here before, he hasn't been living here. We know that because we've been able to chase his digital footprint to Barcelona and London and even the Cayman Islands."

"And you're sure he was there in person, not just his...electronics?" Ben folded his arms on the table and studied them both. "If you're sure, then it's someone who has reappeared in our community in the last two weeks."

"Exactly."

Atlee craned his neck back and stared up at the ceiling for a moment. He wore small spectacles, and of course the suspenders and white shirt. Apparently there were rules about dress as well as everything else. Nora couldn't imagine such a life; but then again, who was she to call someone out on clothing choices? She wore black and black. It was simpler.

"Not in our community," Atlee said. "There's three, maybe four young men who have been in and out, but I was present at their birth. I can assure you that each one is authentically Amish."

"What about the neighboring districts?" Ben asked.

"That is a possibility. I'll have to check with the other bishops, and that's best done in person."

Nora had explained that the countdown clock had started. Every minute that passed, they were one minute closer to disaster.

"I'll set out before daybreak," he assured her. "We're all early risers."

They were in the buggy and on their way back to Ben's when her cell phone went off. She pulled it out and stared at the screen in disbelief. "We need to get to the auction grounds, and we need to hurry."

Chapter 4

Nora knelt beside the body of her partner. He'd been shot in the back at close range. At least he hadn't suffered—the caliber of the slug indicated he'd died instantly.

The local police had found him, and the agency caught wind of it on the police scanners. They'd taken over before the ME could arrive. A helicopter's blades whirred in the distance.

Ben stood behind her, waiting. She was learning that was his way—he didn't talk just to hear his own voice. She appreciated that because she needed a moment to process what had happened. Tate...dead. She'd always assumed he would outlast her, even though he was older. He was that good. So what had happened?

Her mouth felt suddenly dry. Her heart raced as if she'd run to the crime scene, and a distinctive pain radiated from her chest.

The helicopter landed, and one of the agents walked up and said, "I'm sorry, but we need to take him now."

She nodded as if she understood, but the anger

building inside of her made it difficult to think clearly. She literally saw red at the edge of her vision. She would find Dash, and she would kill him. He was worse than an extortionist. He was a thug and a murderer, and he would pay for what he'd done.

"The director said to show you this." The agent handed her an evidence bag holding a note typed on a standard lined index card.

Give me my money and no one else has to die.

"We found it pinned to the back of his jacket." Nora brushed at the tears clouding her vision, then thrust the evidence bag back into his hand. "Anything else?"

"Only that it happened in the last hour, and apparently there were no witnesses...none we've found anyway. So far no leads as to who the perp is."

"It's Dash. There's no doubt about that."

"The director agrees." He handed her a black bag. "Change of clothes, medical supplies, additional ammo, and radios in case the cells stop working."

"Is there any indication that will happen?"

"We're preparing for the worst."

She felt her muscles tighten, as if her body were preparing for an altercation, and walked back to the buggy, Ben dogging her steps.

When they were again on the road, he said, "I'm sorry."

"Tate was a good partner—the best kind of partner. We worked well together."

Ben cleared his throat and kept his attention on the horse a few minutes. Finally he glanced at her and said, "I thought you were working this alone."

"Not what I said..."

"But..."

"I said we were spread thin. Which is why I followed the signal and Tate looked for the bomb. Sometimes it happens like that. You have to split up to complete the mission."

"And now?"

"Now we find Dash, and I kill him."

෨

Ben finally gave up and went to bed. He'd been up since before daybreak and it was now after midnight. Molly would need milking again at five.

Nora turned down the offer of his parents' old room. "I'd only toss all night. Might as well stay up and try to figure out what I've missed."

He left her there, sitting on the couch and staring into space. He thought he might toss and turn, but he was asleep as soon as his head hit the pillow. To say it had been an unusual day for an Amish farmer was an understatement. He rose at his usual time and went out at five to tend to Molly. On his way through the living room, he saw that Nora had covered herself with the sheets he'd left out and curled into a ball on the couch. The room had cooled, and a light breeze stirred through the open windows.

When he came back from the barn she was in the bathroom so he made coffee, slapped half a dozen pieces of bacon in the pan, pulled out eggs and butter and bread and jam.

He felt more than heard her standing behind him, and when he turned and saw her he couldn't help laughing.

"What?"

"Your clothes."

"What's wrong with them?"

"Nothing. It's just..." He turned back toward the stove, tried to stifle the laughter, and failed miserably.

"I'll have you know I've always been a big Notre Dame fan."

"I was more referring to the green leprechaun on your shirt."

She reached past him for the coffee pot. "I'm supposed to blend in. Notre Dame's less than an hour from here. I guess someone at the agency thought this would work."

"Oh, yeah, the college is fine. I was more referring to the glitter."

"What? I'm not a glitter kind of girl?"

"How do you want your eggs?"

"And now you're avoiding the question."

If he was honest, the clothes had thrown him for a loop. She looked more like an *Englisch youngie* than a government agent. Ben was relieved that her mood had lifted from the night before, but he was no fool. Seeing her partner dead, the note from Dash, the hours marching by with no new leads...those things were all weighing on her.

Fifteen minutes later they sat down to eat.

Ben prayed silently, as he always did, thanking God for His provision, for His care.

When he looked up she was staring at him. "Why do you do that?"

"Pray?"

"Yeah. What's the point?"

"To thank Him for all He's given, for watching

over us last night."

"He didn't watch over Tate very well." She stabbed at the eggs as if they were to blame for her partner's death. When she'd finished the meal, she pushed away the plate. "I don't mean to mock you. I admire you, actually."

"You do?"

"But here's the thing. If there is a God, if He's up there and knows everything, then why do you need to tell Him anything? Why do you need to pray?"

"Ah, *ya*. I remember asking my parents that one."

"You did?"

"No one is born believing. We all have to work out our own faith, in our own way."

She hopped up, refilled their mugs, then sat back down and studied him. "So what did your parents say, when you asked them?"

"Oh, they told me that most of the time they know what I'm thinking...that I prefer sweets to vegetables, that I'd like to play ball rather than do chores, that I loved them in spite of my sometimes sharp tone. But even though they knew those things, they still liked to hear it from me. *Mamm* said that part of being in a relationship with one another is communicating those needs and wants and fears and dreams, and that being in a relationship with Gotte is the same."

"They sound like wise parents."

"They were."

She raised an eyebrow and waited.

"They died in a buggy accident. It's been nearly a year."

"I'm sorry." He nodded.

"I guess I thought everyone was off on vacation.

49

So you run this place alone?"

"I do...it's probably too much for one person, but it's the family farm so here I am."

"Brothers and sisters?"

"Nope. All moved to Maine. I was the one that stayed behind."

"Don't most of you people...I mean, isn't it normal..."

"For us to marry? *Ya*. I suppose it is."

"So why haven't you?"

"Guess I haven't met the right person yet. Why haven't you?"

"How do you know I'm not married?"

He must have looked alarmed because she started laughing. "I'm not, and for the same reason I guess."

Which seemed to be all that needed to be said on the subject.

Her mood once again shifted. She reached for her gun, checked and holstered it. There was the woman who had nearly shot him ten hours ago. For reasons he couldn't begin to guess, he felt on more solid ground with Nora the agent than with Nora the Notre Dame football fan.

"You never told me what agency you work for."

"I didn't?"

But instead of answering, she stood up, pushed in her chair, and said, "Thanks for the grub. I'm going to check the perimeter."

He figured that meant he wasn't going to get any more information from her, which was probably just as well. The less he knew the better. What she feared either would or wouldn't happen tonight, and then she'd be gone, and he could get back to his life. Though as he stacked and carried the dishes to the sink he realized he wasn't exactly sure what that life was or why he would be in any hurry to return to it.

༄

Chapter 5

Nora checked the perimeter of the house and outbuildings because she needed something to do, not because she thought she'd find anything. She needed to be out of that kitchen, away from Benjamin Lapp.

So he'd cooked her breakfast.

So what if she couldn't remember the last time anyone had done that, or the last time anyone had looked at her the way he had. She stared down at the glittery green Notre Dame t-shirt she was wearing. Glitter? Seriously?

She walked to the top of the hill, finally got a single bar on her phone, and checked in with headquarters.

No news.

Nothing from Dash. No additional activity.

The hourly emails reminding them where to send the money, reminding them what would happen if they didn't, continued. The director was holding firm. It wasn't about the money. It was about stopping this tonight. Over twenty crews had been sent to crisis points like Shipshewana—all of them small towns, all outside the grid of highway cameras and security drones and facial recognition programs.

The irony was that in recent years there'd been a surge in cyber-insurance policies, mostly purchased by large metropolitan entities—Boston, Nashville, D.C., San Jose, Dallas, Denver, and San Diego. The policies cost as much as thirty million dollars and came with hefty annual premiums.

Some two-bit hacker would demand a five-figure ransom to not do some nefarious deed.

The insurance company would pay because it was the least expensive answer.

The city would collectively offer a sigh of relief— until the next threat came, when it all would be repeated again. That had been the dance for nearly five years now.

But Dash had taken it to an entirely different level.

He'd targeted the small towns, the towns that couldn't and wouldn't purchase such a policy. He'd dared to take on the agency.

Nora trudged back down to the house.

She was sitting in a rocking chair on the porch, cleaning her gun, when Ben walked out.

"Do you have a plan?"

"Yes." She tried not to take offense to the question. "The first thing I need is for you to take me to a car rental place."

"We don't have one."

"What do you mean?"

"I mean Shipshe's too small. The closest car rental place is in South Bend, and I can't go that far in a buggy. In general we only use horses to travel a few miles."

"How do you get around if you need to go farther than a few miles?"

"We hire Englisch drivers. I could walk to the phone shack and call one for you."

She stared at him in disbelief for a moment, but finally shook her head.

"Forget it. Can you take me to the market downtown?"

"Ya. Sure."

When they were nearly to town, she cleared her throat. "Look. You've been a lot of help, but just drop me off."

"Why would I do that?"

"Because this is my job. It isn't yours."

"I get that, but...well, it seems we're in this together."

"How do you figure?"

"You lost a partner last night."

"Are you offering to step up?"

"Sure. Why not? We're already off to a better start today than yesterday. You haven't threatened to shoot me once."

"Give it time."

"See? We get along swell, and besides...if I'm with you, and if Dash is looking for you, I might be able to pick him out of a crowd—like one of those games. You know the ones. What doesn't belong here?"

"That's our Dash all right."

But they didn't find anything at the market, or in the crowds of tourists going from shop to shop, or in the restaurants. Nora gave Ben one of the radios and showed him how to use it, but the only time he called her was to see if she wanted one of JoJo's Pretzels.

They'd agreed to meet back at the buggy at noon. She got there first, and when she saw him hurrying toward her, she knew something had happened.

"It's Atlee. He's got something. Wants us to meet him at the Yoder place, out beyond my farm."

"How do you know that?"

"Atlee told Jeremiah and Caleb, who he knew would be working their booths and would probably see me."

"You people don't even need phones."

"Exactly."

"Though they'd be more efficient."

"You think?"

"Trust me."

ഇം

Ben wasn't sure what he expected to find when they reached the Yoder farm. It was technically in the next church district, so he didn't know the family well, but it was also within two miles of his place so he saw them fairly often passing on the road.

When he arrived at the farm, Atlee was waiting on the porch. "Deborah and the other children have gone next door to her *bruder*'s. Didn't think they needed to hear this."

They walked into a sitting room very much like his own. The only persons there were Thomas Yoder and his oldest daughter. Ben couldn't remember her name.

Atlee introduced everyone.

The girl, Miriam, kept her eyes on the ground.

Thomas explained the situation rather succinctly.

"A man showed up here two weeks ago. Miriam told us that he knew our family in Ohio, and was passing through—needed work and a place to stay. So we put him in the *Dawdi Haus*, and he worked in the fields with me. Man knew nothing about farming, I can tell you that. He disappeared two nights ago. Bishop came to me, asking about strangers we might have seen in the area. I don't know if this is the man you're looking for or not."

Ben glanced at Nora, who was watching the girl intently.

After a moment during which the father offered up nothing additional, Nora tapped her fingers against the arm of the chair she was sitting in. "What did he tell you his name was, Miriam?"

"David. He said his name was David."

"And you thought he was Amish?"

Miriam glanced at her father, then at the floor again.

"Speak the truth to her, child. This is important."

"And what you tell us might save lives. You'd want that, wouldn't you Miriam? You'd want to save people that David might hurt?"

"He'd never do that." She'd been fairly trembling, but now she looked up defiantly.

"He must have seemed like a nice person to you."

"He was. He is." She clutched her arms around her stomach. "I thought he was."

"Is there anything you can tell us? Anything at all?"

"He was *Englisch*—taller than I am by a few inches, thin, and had dark hair. I met him...met him in town. I was there with some girlfriends, and he started talking to us. He seemed...seemed to like me best."

"Did he ask you to say he was Amish?" Ben was floored by the girl's naiveté, but he could see that she was ashamed of what she'd done. In truth she was only guilty of being young and gullible.

"He said it wouldn't hurt anyone to pretend. He said that it would be like a game. We went shopping, and he had money to buy clothes... Amish clothes."

"And then you brought him home." Nora sat forward, her forearms on her knees, her hands clasped together. "Why did he want to come home with you?"

"Said he needed a place to stay a few weeks, and then..." Tears began running down her face. "And then he was going to take me with him. Said he had a place in California and that it looked out over the ocean. That he had family there—his mom and sisters—and I could stay with them."

"Tell me you were not planning to run away with that boy." Her father's face had blanched white.

"I don't know. Maybe. I don't know, *Dat*. It's just... it seemed like my chance to go somewhere different, to be someone different. Is that so wrong?"

When no one spoke, Atlee cleared his throat. "Your parents love you, Miriam, as does your Heavenly Father. What you've done is no worse than what all of us have done at one time or another. Trusting someone you shouldn't, and recognizing that mistake, is part and parcel of growing up."

"So you're not mad at me?"

"No one's mad," Atlee assured her.

Ben wasn't so sure. Thomas looked pretty steamed, but then what parent wouldn't be? No doubt that came from fear—fear over what could have happened.

"Did he hurt you, Miriam?" Nora's face had taken on a particular fierceness that Ben hadn't seen before.

"Nein."

"You're certain about that? Because if he has, we can get you to a doctor."

"We only...only kissed a few times."

"Okay. Is there anything else...anything at all that you can tell us?"

Nora's patience surprised Ben. She'd apparently worked with timid witnesses before, though probably none of those had been Amish teenagers.

"He had a gun. He told me it wasn't loaded and that he just had it for when he was hitching rides, so no one would try any funny stuff."

"And a cell phone?"

"*Ya.*"

"All right. I'm going to get a sketch artist our here in the next hour. I'd like you to work with her." Nora stood, thanked Atlee and Thomas and Miriam, and motioned to Ben that they could go. They were halfway to the door when Miriam spoke up, her voice pleading.

"Do you really think he would hurt anyone?"

"I know he would." Nora walked back to the couch and pulled up the sleeve of her t-shirt, revealing the pressure bandage that Ben had changed that morning. "He did this—yesterday, and he also killed a man."

Miriam was visibly shaking now. "He made me promise not to tell. He told me it was our secret."

"What? What were you not supposed to tell?"

"About the lake. About the little garden shed by the lake."

ॐ

Two hours later Ben and Nora stood on the old fishing dock at Lake Shipshewana. They'd found the shed where Dash had stored his supplies.

"How did he even find this place?"

"The man is resourceful."

"What do you think he was using it for?"

"Maybe to store his electronic equipment, even a portable server. That would explain why his signal eventually bounced to this area, which he would have known that we'd see. He wanted us here. Wanted us close but not too close."

"Why?"

"Because it shows his superiority."

Ben could practically feel the frustration building inside her. It was almost as if he'd known her for years instead of hours. She'd called in a tech crew and they were going over the shed, which couldn't have been larger than six feet by six. It was amazing no one had stumbled on it.

One of the techs poked his head out. "You're going to want to see this."

They hurried over. The shed itself was dark, but the men were holding different sorts of light instruments in their hands that revealed blues, reds, and greens throughout the shed...as if colored paint had been splashed across the workbench and floor. Nora took one look and stormed out of the shed, to the end of the pier, and pulled out her phone. When she finished the call, she motioned to Ben.

He hurried with her toward the buggy. "What just happened?"

"Bomb residue. He's doing it, Ben. He took advantage of that young girl, inserted himself into this community, and used her to provide an alibi to help him keep his secrets. He brought her out here and had her act as his lookout. He convinced her that he was doing important work, something that would ensure their future together in California."

"Let me guess...this had nothing to do with California."

"Nothing. He was making a bomb, and Miriam? Miriam was covering for him, and she never knew it."

"So what do we do?"

"We stop him. We find him and we stop him before that bomb he's created has a chance to detonate."

Chapter 6

They spent the next two hours going over their plan—studying a layout of the park and discussing contingencies. The director would send more people if he could, if the intel warranted it. Twenty different disaster scenarios in twenty different towns at the same time. Dash hadn't been bluffing. Confirmation of sites similar to the fishing shed was coming in from all over the country. Once again, the agency was running a step behind.

Chances were that help wouldn't be coming. They should proceed as if they were on their own.

They arrived back in town two hours before the concert was set to begin, splitting up and observing the park site from every angle, looking for anything suspicious, anything that would indicate exactly where or how he planned to detonate the explosive.

They came up with nothing. The park was clean.

The sketch artist had finished working with Miriam and had forwarded a composite sketch of Dash. Nora uploaded it to her phone, and they showed it to anyone who might have seen him.

Her director had shared pertinent information with the local police, along with a warning that a dangerous suspect was in the area. Nora didn't bother providing those details to the people she showed the sketch. They didn't need to know, and she didn't want to alarm them when this could be a mere distraction perpetrated by Dash. The director thought it was real. The intelligence confirmed it was real, as did what they'd found in the shed.

But Dash was wily. He could have planted all of this and killed Tate. He could also be far away by now, planning something much worse. No one had seen a man fitting Dash's description.

No one had seen anything out of place.

Nora released the clip from her gun, checked that it was full, slapped the clip back in, and racked the slide.

"We'll find him," Ben assured her.

"You don't know that."

"I do." He nodded as if it were possible to become more convinced by saying it. "We will."

They'd met back at the buggy and taken a moment to arm up, which equaled Nora checking the gun she'd been carrying all day and slipping an extra clip into the back pocket of her jeans.

"Still have your radio?"

Ben held it up and wiggled it back and forth. "You?"

She patted the front of her denim vest. She'd feel better in her Kevlar, but you couldn't walk around a Saturday night concert in Kevlar and not alarm people. "Let's go."

They were running out of time.

In spite of the information her director had shared with the local police, the decision was made to go ahead with the evening's festivities. Local officials were skeptical that any sort of terrorist attack could happen in their town. They'd put their entire police force on duty for the event, but other than Tate's dead body they'd found nothing to concern them. Perhaps he'd simply been in the wrong place at the wrong time.

Someone was making announcements over the large speakers set up around the park. "Music starts in twenty minutes, folks. Get your refreshments, grab the kids, and find your seats. We'll start at seven o'clock sharp."

Nora exchanged a glance with Ben. Twenty minutes. Whatever was going to happen would happen soon.

They walked side-by-side through the crowd and stopped near the center. Standing back to back they pivoted in a circle, watching, looking, needing to separate the madman from the crowd.

He was there.

She knew it as surely as Ben knew they would find him. Why couldn't she see him? Why couldn't she stop what was about to happen? She hadn't been able to save Tate, but she would avenge his murder. All her training ached to fire the shot that would stop this.

As her frustration built to a near crescendo, she found herself doing something she hadn't done in many years. In her heart, she cried out to God. Surely He would save these people. He wouldn't allow such destruction to happen.

Would He?

If she'd hoped to hear a still small voice, she was

disappointed.

No angel appeared at her side directing her right or left.

No heavenly chorus broke into song declaring what her path should be.

She broke out of her reverie when a small boy standing next to her grabbed his mother's hand. Amish, wearing the same clothes as his father only in miniature, he looked up at his momma—his mamm as Ben said. The smile on the child's face was practically angelic, and his voice, though pleading, hadn't slipped into a whine. "You promised. Remember? If I ate all my dinner, if I was good, I could have a snow cone. I've been good. Right?"

The mother laughed. "Ya, you've been very gut."

"Snow cones," Ben said, his voice a whisper in her ear.

"What?"

"Snow cones." He turned south. "I've never...I've never seen a snow cone truck in Shipshe before."

They broke into a run at the same moment, dodging families, feinting left and right.

The snow cone truck was parked near the stage. A long line of children waited patiently for their turn. Nora nearly tripped over a toddler. A parent called out, "Hey, slow down before you hurt someone," and Dash looked up from the trailer's window. His eyes met hers, and even from the distance of thirty yards she saw a smile twitch at the corner of his mouth.

Then he was gone.

Adrenaline coursed through her veins and she ran harder, faster, hitting the back steps of the trailer at the same time that Ben did.

No one was there. Dash had fled. She scanned the room and saw jars of syrup, chests of ice, a cash drawer, and beneath the counter a box flashing three minutes.

Not enough time.

She couldn't call in a bomb squad. She didn't know how to dismantle it.

Ben was standing behind her, his breathing ragged.

"Get them out of here, Ben. Get them all away from this trailer."

She darted out the back, spotted Dash crossing the main road, and took off after him.

၉

The red numbers flashed 2:55, 2:54, 2:53.

Ben's life had come to this. His purpose was in the small faces looking up to the window, waiting for a cold syrupy treat on a summer evening in August.

The woman standing at the front of the line with three children looked up in alarm as he tore around the corner of the trailer. He picked up the smallest, tossed the child into her arms, and tucked the other two under his arms as if they were no heavier than the scarecrows his mamm once kept in her garden.

"There's a bomb! Run! Everyone run!"

Later he would puzzle over why they believed him—an Amish man, snatching up children and screaming of Armageddon.

He would never completely understand the why or even the how of it, but they did believe him.

People started running—Amish and Englisch—

helping one another to their feet and urging each other to move faster. A great wave of humanity all seeking a safe harbor. They left behind blankets and dinners and baskets and baby strollers. They left behind the things of their lives that didn't really matter, the things that could be purchased again. They grabbed their loved ones and their friends and the strangers beside them, and they moved with great urgency to the opposite side of the park.

He'd stayed toward the back after handing the children over to their father and pushing them to the north, telling them to go—to run. Ben's mind tried to calculate how much time had passed since he stepped out of the trailer.

What were the red numbers flashing now?

Had they moved everyone in time?

His eyes scanned the sea of possessions in front of him, needing to be sure that no one was left. A woman's voice came over the speakers telling everyone to remain calm, and sirens were blaring in the distance.

And then the red, glowing numbers on the small black box must have reached zero because there was an explosion, and people were screaming, and something was running down the side of his face. And the spot where the snow cone trailer had been was nothing more than a wall of flame.

၉

Nora kept up with Dash until he ducked behind the Davis Mercantile.

She had gained a lot of ground, but he was a few seconds ahead of her, and when she turned the corner she saw only a quilt shop window, closed stores, empty parking spaces. Everyone was at the park. She'd heard the explosion as she was running but hadn't turned back. She couldn't turn back. He would do it again, and it would be worse. She was not going to let that happen.

Her radio squeaked—Ben asking where she was. She reached up with her left and turned the volume all the way down. She led with her right, the bicep once again throbbing, the gun in front of her and chest high. She walked down the alley behind the building, heel to toe, silent except for the sound of her beating heart raging in her ears.

He'd stashed a car there, an old beat up Volkswagen. He looked up as he slipped the key into the lock, and again he smiled.

"Step away from the car."

"Shouldn't you be over there? Saving people?" The smile slipped away, like a mask might fall off an actor, and she saw him for what he was—a bitter, frightened, and angry man.

"I said, step away from the car."

"You people. Your money is so important to you that you'd rather risk the lives of hundreds, of thousands..."

"Both hands in the air." She closed the gap between them to ten feet and pointed the gun like they'd first trained her—center of mass.

"I was trying to keep you safe. I was trying to wake you up."

"With a bomb in a public park?"

"You should be thanking me. Now you see how vulnerable you are. Now everyone will see. These people think they're safe because they're in a small town, but no one's safe. Not anymore."

"Dash, I need you to step away from the car."

"A terrorist doesn't need to show up at a park in a snow cone truck with a bomb. All he needs is a laptop and a programmer smart enough to hack into your systems and drop the grid."

"So why the bomb?"

"To wake you up, and so you'd know that what I do next, I do not do lightly."

"You're not going to do anything. It's over."

"That bomb might have killed a few hundred, but when I hack into the electrical grid in the northwest or the dam controls at Hoover or the 9-1-1 system in New York, thousands will die, and that will be your fault, agent. You should have just paid the ransom." And with his smile firmly once again in place, he reached into the pocket of his jacket.

She didn't even hesitate. She pulled the trigger.

Chapter 7

Ben stood beside her as two medics loaded Dash onto a stretcher, cuffed his hands to the sidebars, and walked his stretcher to the helicopter.

"You didn't kill him."

"You sound surprised."

"I am—a little."

"Maybe you're a good influence on me."

"Or maybe you decided your agency could get more information out of him alive. Maybe your mind won out over your grief."

She turned and smiled at him. "You're a pretty smart guy, Ben Lapp."

"Am I now?"

"Seem to be."

She waved away the medic approaching her. The pressure bandage had come lose sometime during the last hour and blood once again seeped through her shirt, but it would keep. She wasn't going to bleed out because of it. Once she saw Dash handed over to the director, she'd go to medical and have it stitched up properly. She did accept the bottle of water that Ben offered and slugged down half of it.

"Thanks."

"Gem gschehne."

"What does that mean?"

"It means you're welcome."

They walked to the end of the alley, where they could see the park.

"No one was killed? You're sure?"

"Several guys on the volunteer fire crew are Amish. They told me the worst of it was a broken ankle, two sprains, and a couple of near heart attacks."

"Not great."

"Nein."

"But not bad..." She raised her right hand and he slapped his palm against it. "We make a good team."

"Do we?"

"You should think about coming to work with the agency."

His laugh was full, rich, enticing. "You should think about farming."

Someone called out to her, she turned toward the helicopter, raised her hand to indicate she'd heard, and then turned back to Ben. "Thank you, for everything."

"You already said that." And then he surprised both of them by stepping closer, slipping his hand under her chin and kissing her ever so gently on the lips.

"Wow." She stepped back, unable to stop the smile that was spreading across her face and feeling like a teenager on a first date. "I didn't see that coming."

"Take care of yourself. Promise?"

"I always do."

She didn't look back. She'd spent so much of her life leaving people. She couldn't bear to look back. So instead she jogged to the helicopter, grabbed the hand reaching down for her, and felt herself being pulled up and in. She clipped into the harness, and as the helicopter rose, she glanced down.

Ben remained at the end of the alley, one hand raised to cover his eyes against the setting sun, the other waving.

They flew over the park, which was a jumble of left-behind possessions and crime scene tape and evidence waiting to be gathered. But no bodies, and for that she was grateful.

The park area grew smaller until it resembled a child's toy.

෨

Ben heard from her only one time after that.

He'd checked the recorder at the phone shack to see if his bruder had called. He was planning a fall trip to Maine to try the fishing and to consider a move. He'd held onto the past long enough. He was ready, even eager, to move forward.

"This message is for Ben Lapp."

Just hearing her voice brought a smile to his lips.

He sat on the single stool in the phone shack, staring at the recorder, willing her to make the message a long one.

"Ben, this is Nora. I want you to know that what we did, well it stopped the others. He'd set up a cascading protocol—he wanted to be the first, the event that started it all. When he didn't make the call, the others dispersed to the wind. We've caught about half of them." There was a pause in the recording, and he could hear the sound of cars and busses and people behind her. "Thank you—again. And say hello to Molly for me."

Ben was tempted to replay the message, but he didn't need to. It was good to know that it had ended well, that they had done what needed to be done. He was smiling as he pushed delete on the recorder. Settling his hat on his head, he walked out into the September sunshine and a new chapter in his life.

The End

☙

Author's Note

This book is dedicated to my readers, who are quite patient with me when I stray off into other genres. To date, I've published Amish romances, Amish mysteries, Christian suspense, "clean" suspense, and dystopian novels. Many of you have faithfully read where ever my attention wanders. Thank you for honoring me with your time and your wonderful reviews.

I'd like to thank my co-authors in *Summer of Suspense*, where this story first appeared. You were a wonderful group of ladies to work with and I'm still super proud that we made the *USA Today* Bestseller list with that collection. I also owe a debt of gratitude to my dad, who taught me to critically consider all things before I embrace them.

As is always the case, I owe a large debt to my pre-readers: Kristy and Janet. Teresa, I am so glad that you are my editor, cover designer, and formatter on this one. You're amazing.

I've always been a fan of conspiracy theories—they're simply fun to bat around. As far as technology, for me the verdict is still out. If I should decide to embrace an "off-the-grid" lifestyle, I'll send you all a message via parchment.

And finally ...always giving thanks to God the Father for everything, in the name of our Lord Jesus Christ (Ephesians 5:20).

Blessings,
Vannetta

Midnight Strike

Cyber Division, Book 2

Dedicated to
My Family

While this novella is set against the real backdrop of Dallas, Texas, the characters as well as the community are fictional. There is no intended resemblance between the characters in this book and any real persons. As with any work of fiction, I've taken license in some areas of research as a means of creating the necessary circumstances for my characters. My research was thorough; however, it would be impossible to be completely accurate in details and descriptions. Therefore, any inaccuracies portrayed in this book are completely due to fictional license.

Contents

"Say to those with fearful hearts,
Be strong, do not fear."
~Isaiah 35:4

"We've arranged a civilization in which
most crucial elements profoundly depend
on science and technology."
~Carl Sagan

Chapter One

Nora Brooks fidgeted with the clasp of her necklace and wondered how much longer she had to endure the small talk. Nylah tossed her a pointed look, as if to say, *don't even think about ditching us.* Nora and Nylah had come up through the academy together, but friendship only went so far—even friendship cemented in staving off national crisis.

The problem was that Nylah had found Curtis.

Curtis, in and of himself, wasn't an issue. In fact, he was a member of the cyber task force, too—only on the tech side rather than the operational side. He and Nylah made a cute couple.

The problem with people in love was that they thought everyone else should be in love, or at least in a relationship, *at least trying,* as Nylah had so succinctly put it to her the night before.

Which was how Nora ended up in a five-star restaurant, sitting next to a guy who researched viruses, trying to make small talk about the Washington Nationals.

Nora didn't care about baseball.

She had no interest in viruses—other than the computer kind.

And she absolutely hated small talk.

Nylah's eyes widened, then she shook her head in disappointment.

At first Nora thought her best friend had read her mind, then she realized Curtis was watching someone over her shoulder.

Nora turned around to see Randall Goodwin striding across the restaurant, definitely zoning in on their table. She almost sighed with relief. From the look on his face they were facing a national emergency. Was it wrong to prefer that over the awkwardness of a blind date? Fine, then she was a terrible person. So be it.

She stood before he even reached the table.

Randall nodded at Curtis and Nylah before stepping closer to Nora. "The director is waiting outside."

She knew she didn't have to explain to her friends, and they would make up some excuse for her date—she couldn't remember his name at the moment, but that didn't matter.

She strode out of the restaurant with Randall.

"Nice pantsuit, Brooks."

"Save it, Goodwin."

The director's Suburban was parked under the portico. His security personnel opened the back door. Nora and Randall hopped in and the vehicle pulled away, tires spitting rain from the wet DC streets. They were stuck in that gray space between winter and spring. Everything seemed cold, wet, and dreary.

Jason Anderson had recently turned fifty-three. He had short-cropped gray hair and a scar that ran from his left eye to his jawline.

Nora had heard rumors about how the director had earned the scar. The stories ranged from Soviet spies infiltrating the White House to homegrown terrorists he'd battled hand-to-hand on top of the Empire State Building. In each version, regardless the details, the perpetrator ended up on a slab at the morgue and the director ended up with the scar.

The director studied them both, then offered an apology. "Sorry to interrupt your evening off."

"Actually, I owe you. Blind dates apparently aren't my thing."

Streetlights pierced the tinted windows enough for her to make out her boss's features. If the job was taking a toll on him, she couldn't tell. He seemed to live and breathe cyber security. Perhaps that was why he understood her so well. Though there was a pinched look around his eyes this evening, something that only occurred when he was extremely concerned about a situation.

"You're both going to Dallas. A Level 4 event began six hours ago."

"Why weren't we told six hours ago?"

"You weren't on rotation tonight. Taylor and Santos were. They were briefed and caught a domestic flight to DFW. The plane experienced a technical issue, and they were diverted to Atlanta. They're trying to catch another flight out, but haven't had any luck."

Randall shifted in his seat. "Any chance their detour was related to the Dallas event?"

"You're suggesting the cyberbugs were aware of our plans and had the ability to disrupt them—which before tonight we considered impossible. Now? Our analysts put that probability at 82%."

"Tell me we're not driving." Nora didn't mind driving, but DC to Dallas would take twenty hours. Whatever was happening in Dallas would be over before they got there.

"We're putting you on a military transport. If they manage to infiltrate that, we have bigger problems than Dallas."

An hour later they'd boarded a C-20 Gulfstream naval jet that would take them to the Grand Prairie Armed Forces Reserve Complex, a former naval air station.

"It's a twenty minute drive to Dallas from Grand Prairie." Randall made no attempt to stifle a yawn. "Better catch some sleep while you can."

They were the only two passengers on the plane, a testament to the director's pull. Randall put his seat all the way back and stretched his legs out in front of him. At six foot four, he usually complained about flying because he never had enough leg space.

He was young and cocky, which Nora thought came from his father. Michael Goodwin had enjoyed a long NFL career as a tight end. Randall assured her that both traits were from his mom, who'd managed to raise five boys on her own since their father was gone for months at a time. Dad had gone on to make a couple million in the stock market and now had his own consulting firm and Mom was a biochemist, so Randall's superior IQ could have come from either parent. His skin was a light brown, and at twenty-seven his physique remained toned and muscular. Women seemed drawn to him. All those things did nothing to mitigate his cockiness.

"Have you studied this file at all?"

"Sure."

"Looks like a cascading attack across transportation, communication, utilities, and medical."

"Which is the reason it's a Level 4."

"Transportation could stop air travel, ground travel, all traffic cams and lights..."

"A real mess in a metroplex the size of Dallas. Then with comms out you have no cell service."

"Which means no 9-1-1." Nora suddenly understood the director's concern. Most threats they dealt with hit one, possibly two sectors. They hadn't seen anything this invasive. "Utilities means no gas and electric."

"Not as big a deal as it might be in the north. No one is going to freeze to death in Dallas, even in January."

"And medical. How does that fit in? It seems... like an overreach."

"Most hospitals are hooked up to the grid like everyone else. Tonya told me—"

"Tonya, the girl you dated exactly twice?"

Randall flashed her a smile. "The same. She was a pharmacist at Johns Hopkins. Told me they can't dispense a pill on their own. It's all done through a giant computer. Doctors put in their codes and the machine dumps out the meds."

"They must have a backup plan in case the system goes down."

"They have a generator."

"Which won't help a bit if our perp has hacked into the actual system." Nora's mind scanned the list of cyber-terrorists they'd encountered over the last ten years. Most were behind bars, but it seemed that for every one they arrested, two more sprouted up. "I can't think of a single cyberbug who has the ability to do something like this."

Randall stuffed the small airplane pillow behind his head. He was really going to go to sleep. She couldn't believe it.

She nudged him with her foot.

"Any idea what we're facing here?"

"You're the experienced agent on our team. What do you think it is?"

She scanned back over the three pages, then closed the file and stared out the window. "No single group has the capability of doing something like this."

"Which means..."

"Which means it's a coalition. Something has prompted our cyberbugs to work together."

"All the more reason to get some sleep."

Ten minutes later Randall was snoring.

Sometimes she envied his ability to shut everything off.

It didn't work that way for her. It never had.

෨

Randall woke when they began their descent. He walked to the back of the plane, used the lavatory, and splashed water on his face. Then he snagged two cups of coffee from the galley.

Nora hadn't slept. She never slept on planes. They'd once been sent on assignment to China. She'd stayed awake through the entire flight.

He'd joined the agency four years ago, and he'd

risen quickly because he understood both the technical and operational sides of cyber security.

Learned to code before turning ten years old.

Received offers from MIT and Caltech.

Randall wasn't a genius, but he wasn't that far from it. For reasons he couldn't fathom, computer code was like a language he'd spoken from birth. After joining the agency, he lasted less than a year on the analytical side. He never had been able to abide sitting behind a desk. Operations had an opening, and he jumped at it.

He'd been assigned three different partners in four years, and Nora Brooks was by far the best.

Randall understood code.

Nora understood people.

She had an intuitive nature that put her ahead of everyone else. Or maybe she was just able to think like a criminal. Whatever the reason, the woman was quickly becoming a legend within the agency, and she didn't even know it. She seemed to have no life other than stopping the next cyberattack. Her thoughts were always on the cyberbugs.

He'd almost laughed when he saw Nora sitting at the elegant table. Not that she wasn't elegant—in her blue pantsuit and heels, and with her short red hair cascading around her face....Nora belonged anywhere she wanted to. No, it was more that sitting at the table crowded with china, she'd reminded him of a caged jaguar.

"Why did you change your clothes?" He asked as he pushed the cup of coffee into her hands.

"Seriously?"

"I didn't even know you owned anything other than black."

"Well, I didn't see any reason to make you privy to the contents of my wardrobe, Randall."

"Wardrobe. Ha. That's funny. I don't think you can call five identical pairs of black pants and five black tops a wardrobe."

He liked to dress well. Not too well, no need drawing attention to yourself, but pressed slacks, medium starch in his shirts, high-end quality. Dolce & Gabbana was currently his favorite brand.

"This came in while you were catching your beauty sleep."

Randall accepted the tablet from her.

```
DFW Metropolitan Area
Level 4 Cyberattack: Code Name Artemis
0300 Update
Motor vehicle accidents up 12%
9-1-1 response time delayed by an
average of eight minutes
Rolling brown outs across municipal
grid
Medical systems compromised
```

"How bad is the media response?"

"They don't know yet."

"How can they not know yet?"

The plane hit an air pocket and bounced. Randall reflexively grabbed the arm rests. Nora didn't seem to notice.

"They're scrambling. Everyone's scrambling, so they haven't put it together."

"My granny would notice a 12% increase in car wrecks caused by traffic lights not working."

"Nope. Your granny would be in bed."

"Granny has some issues sleeping."

"Granny would be playing solitaire, maybe, but she wouldn't be out cruising the streets of Dallas."

Randall frowned at the tablet. "I thought cyberbugs wanted to make the biggest bang for the buck—the most chaos for the code. Why do this in the middle of the night when apparently no one is noticing?"

"Because this is the warm-up."

Nora took the tablet and stored it in her backpack. Only Nora could make a black backpack look cool. Randall wondered how it would look with his $400 poplin dress shirt and quickly dismissed the idea.

"Still no ransom?" he asked.

"No."

"Then it's some psycho, like the bug in San Francisco who thought it was his job to help push California over into the ocean...as if a cyberattack could move land mass. That guy was a nut and so is this one."

"You're showing your prejudice, Randall. No one said this was a guy."

"I was using the term generically."

"Uh-huh."

"Women can be psychos, too, and they can be cyberbugs."

"Equal opportunity."

"Exactly."

Nora flashed him a smile, and Randall enjoyed the fleeting thought that this was going to be fun.

Then the captain came over the speakers. "Folks. We have a problem."

୧

Chapter Two

Nora and Randall crowded into the cockpit. She had no idea what the array of read-outs and switches and lights meant. She didn't want to know. She wanted the plane to deliver them where she needed to be—on the ground in Grand Prairie, Texas—so she could do her job.

"The computer is telling us that the winds are too high."

"But they're not..." Nora leaned toward a read-out positioned between the pilot and co-pilot. "Says we have a 4 mph westerly wind."

"There was some turbulence earlier," Randall pointed out.

"Air pocket." The co-pilot looked to be in her twenties. Nora marveled that she was experienced enough to fly a thirty-seven million dollar jet, but perhaps that was simply her own prejudice asserting itself. Since she'd turned thirty-eight, everyone seemed younger and dangerously inexperienced.

"Could your system have been hacked?" Randall ran a hand over the top of his head. "Are there any other indications that might have happened?"

"None." The pilot was older and had a respectable amount of gray in his hair. "It's more likely that someone has infiltrated from the other end—say, the weather instrumentation on the airfield."

Nora was willing to bet he'd served overseas in active combat. She was willing to bet all their lives that he could land the jet without instrumentation.

"Can you override it?"

"No."

"But you can turn it all off?"

"Excuse me?" For the first time the pilot turned to look at her, white eyebrows arched over bright blue eyes.

"The instrumentation...you can turn it off, override it, go in dark."

"I can, but why would I?"

"Because they don't want us landing. They've already rerouted the team in front of us."

"I don't have the authority to make that decision."

"I do." Nora pulled a card from her pocket. Embossed on it was a single twelve digit number followed by several symbols.

The pilot glanced at it, punched it into a machine and received a green light. "All right. It's your call, but I suggest you buckle up."

As they left the cockpit, she heard him conveying information to the air traffic control tower in Grand Prairie.

"Why don't I have one of those cards?" Randall dropped back into his seat and cinched his seatbelt.

Nora put her hands against the bulkhead and stretched like a cat after a long nap. When she heard a satisfying pop in her spine, she sat and buckled.

"Nora, did you hear me? Why don't I have one of those cards?"

Instead of answering, she nodded toward the window where the ground was rushing up at what seemed like an impossible speed.

ço

Forty minutes later a lieutenant was speeding them down Interstate 30 toward downtown Dallas. Randall was staring at the update on the tablet's screen. Nora had glanced at it—one glance had been enough. Malfunctions in every category were increasing. The media would notice it soon. Fortunately, it was still a few hours shy of sunrise. Most people would be asleep. They had a little time to get ahead of this.

The driver exited the freeway. They practically flew past the grassy knoll, then the infamous Sixth Street Book Depository, circled around Kennedy's Memorial, and finally stopped in front of a nondescript brick building. It looked rather out of place amidst the newly built glass towers surrounding them—more than a dozen buildings at close to a thousand feet tall. Two dozen more midsized structures crowded around those. Businesses interspersed with hotels and condos filled out the skyline, and just beyond that lay the arts district. She'd read that downtown Dallas now had close to 15,000 full time residents, but the place looked deserted.

It wouldn't stay that way.

A military guard opened the door as they approached. Three more stood at attention at critical positions in the lobby. Unfortunately, no one expected the person or persons behind this attack to stride in through the front door of the building. If only things were that simple.

Nora was surprised when the guard assigned to them ushered them into the elevator and selected the top floor. Usually cyber ops were situated in the basement, as if being underground could protect them.

The floor they stepped out on contained an open workspace dotted with a vast array of computer stations. No cubicle walls. No corner offices. If there were shades for the floor to ceiling windows that rimmed the room, they were retracted. She walked straight to the far windows and stared out over the skyline.

Dallas in late January was nearly as dreary as DC. Fortunately it was warmer, though it was predicted to turn cloudy with rain later in the day. Weather didn't tend to affect cyber events, but it could make first responders' jobs more difficult. Hopefully it wouldn't come to that.

Even as she watched, a rolling brownout started to the south, shifted to the west, then north, then east. By the time whatever was happening reached full circle, the electricity was back on to the south.

"Impressive."

She turned and studied Randall. "And no doubt this little show of power is for our benefit."

"Actually, they've been doing that all night." The man who stepped forward must have been closer to seven feet than six. He had a shiny bald head, thin frame, and designer glasses. "Adam Quinn, chief analyst for the Greater Dallas Metropolitan Area Cyber Task Force."

"That's a mouth full." Randall shook his hand, as did Nora.

"Bring us up to date." Nora didn't expect to hear anything new, but she liked to be briefed by someone on the ground. Occasionally a small detail emerged that hadn't been deemed worthy to make it into the report.

Nora and Randall followed Quinn to a workstation in the center of the room. She hadn't noticed before that it was on a raised platform—probably no more than six inches higher than the rest of the workspace, but it was enough to give him a view of what every person was doing on every computer terminal. It was, quite literally, a command center.

Quinn began pulling up graphs and mentioning similarities of the current attack to previous ones—Red October and WannaCry and Petya. Randall asked if he could push some of the infected code to an open work station, and after a brief hesitation Quinn agreed.

Nora saw a familiar gleam in her partner's eyes. He was in his element when he could play with code while on site in the middle of an active cyberattack. It was like the trifecta of workplace satisfaction for him.

Nora watched Randall slip into the workstation chair. He'd be occupied for at least an hour, maybe more, before he could give her any type of report. She turned to Quinn. "Mind if I speak to your people?"

Quinn looked almost amused at the idea. "Not at all, but I can assure you that everything they've seen or heard was in the report I forwarded to you earlier."

"I'd like the names of everyone who has worked on this particular attack, including but not limited to those who have gone off shift."

"My crew doesn't go off shift." Quinn's smile

was tight. He crossed his arms, stared out at his team, then back at her. Whatever politeness was there when they'd first walked in was gone. This was his turf, and she'd offended him. She wasn't sure how and didn't particularly care.

"I'll get you the names."

"Fine. I'll let you know if I need anything else."

There were probably thirty people in the room. She started with the ones who looked the worst—rumpled clothes, hair disheveled, eyes already red from staring into a monitor. They would have been there the longest, if Quinn's response was any indication.

Let Randall play with the code and look for an electronic signature. Let him work that half of the puzzle. It wasn't Nora's field of expertise, and she'd only be in the way. But people? People she could read, and she was willing to bet that someone in this room had heard or seen something they didn't think was worth passing on. Cases had turned on less.

ʚ

Randall felt the familiar buzz of adrenaline coursing through his veins. Every programmer—every coder—had a signature, something akin to a digital fingerprint. It was usually something small: a favorite tweak to the last line of every section of code, a way of embedding commands, a habit that was comfortable and always worked so why change it. Randall could spot such signatures like a bloodhound could sniff out a rabbit. Signatures literally leapt off the page to him, almost as if they were embossed on top of the code. He glanced up, saw that Nora had completed her circuit around the room, and motioned her over.

She crossed her arms and rested her backside against his table. "Want to take a break?"

"Why would I need a break?"

"Because you've been at it two hours." Nora tilted her head toward the windows. "Nearly sunrise."

"Huh." If you'd asked him, he would have guessed twenty minutes had passed. "I want you to look at something."

He turned back toward the terminal, pulled up four windows with four different sections of code.

"What am I looking at?"

"The four prong attack. Remember? Transportation, communication, utilities..."

"And medical."

"Exactly. First look at each section individually."

"You've found a signature."

"Within the section."

"But they don't match."

"Across the board? No. They don't." He spun around to face her, elbows resting on the chair's arms, fingers steepled. "It's a coalition, just like you said."

"Does anyone else know this?"

"Doubtful. They've been playing catch-up all night, and I'm willing to bet Quinn put a different analyst on each section of code. They wouldn't have thought to compare yet. Plus, within each section, the signature grows increasingly harder to decipher."

"They're playing with us."

"They are."

"That's one thing you can count on with cyberbugs. They want everyone to know they're the smartest person in the room."

Randall sat up straighter in his chair. "We have company."

A man had wheeled into the room, followed by an entourage of secretaries, assistants, and even secret service if Randall was reading the group correctly.

"Governor Abbott." Nora lowered her voice. "Forty-eighth governor of Texas. Republican. Roman Catholic. Wife was a school teacher then a principal. First governor in a wheelchair since George Wallace."

"How do you know so much about him?'

Nora shrugged.

"Was he born disabled?"

"Oak tree fell on him while he was jogging."

"Paralyzed him?"

"It did. He sued both the homeowner and the tree service company and won. Financially he doesn't need to work, and he certainly doesn't need the hassles of public office."

"So why does he do it?"

"Because he's one of the good guys." Nora had been half sitting on the desk where Randall was working. Now she stood as the governor rolled toward them.

"Nora, it's good to see you again."

"Again?" Randall shook the governor's hand as he introduced himself. "I wasn't aware that you and my partner knew one another."

"Sure. Nora helped us out with that coordinated attack last year."

"Where was I?"

"Vacation in Maui." Nora turned her attention back toward Abbott. It was obvious from her body language that she respected the man. That was enough for Randall. If she said the governor was one of the good guys, then he was.

"Randall has discovered new information about the perps."

"Why wasn't I aware of these findings?" Quinn had managed to sneak up behind them, no small feat for a guy of his height.

"He was just showing me the data. I'll have him go over it with your analysts."

Abbott held up a hand. "First I'd like you three plus Quinn's top people to meet with my staff."

Nora started to protest, but before she could do more than pull in a deep breath, Abbott wheeled closer. "Nora, I remember you don't like being pulled away from the action, but I promise we'll be brief."

Since there wasn't an office to retreat to, Abbott pulled everyone into the far northeast corner of the office space. Quinn's people scurried to alternate workstations.

"I want to introduce you to Shelly Rodriguez, my senior advisor. Shelly, catch everyone up."

A Hispanic woman with long black hair pulled back off her shoulders and dressed in a trim black skirt and jacket stepped forward. "Every municipality in Texas has been sent a Code Alamo, and all have responded then gone dark."

"I've never heard of Code Alamo," Quinn muttered.

"You were on a need to know basis, and until now—you didn't need to know." Though Abbott sat in a wheelchair, effectively rendering him four feet tall, he had no trouble meeting the gaze of every person in their corner. "Code Alamo is a program Shelly and I developed after the cyberattack last August. Each municipality is instructed to disconnect from state-wide and national networks. No data in and no data out."

"You built a Faraday cage." It was a beautiful solution. Why had no one thought of it before? But then again, Randall recognized that few municipalities would willingly go off-line. It would affect everything from cell phone reception to weather reports to state and national resources. It wouldn't work for an extended period of time. But it might work long enough.

"The message was hand delivered, and the message to reconnect will also be hand delivered," Shelly explained. "Extreme threats require equally extreme measures, and we believe this will be an effective one. Our municipalities will be working in the dark, but we believe they can handle whatever comes their way. We're as good as the people who work for us, and we believe they are very good."

And there it was, the reason local leaders would be willing to follow such extreme orders. Abbott and his people respected the locals and trusted they could take care of things in the interim.

"We're here to be updated—in person—on the current status of the Dallas attack, and also to let you know what we've done to protect the larger integrity of our state's systems." Shelly nodded at Abbott, then took two steps back.

"Any questions?" Abbott waited the space of thirty seconds, an uncomfortably long pause which put everyone's attention directly on him. Once he had their eyes and ears trained on his next move, he sat straighter in his chair. "Well, I have one. As far as we can tell, this attack has been limited to Dallas. Why? Obviously whoever is behind it has the ability to go to the next level. Why aren't they attacking at a national level?"

"Actually, they are." Nora clasped her hands behind her back. "Someone intercepted the first team that was dispatched here."

"Have they breached TSA or a single airliner?" Abbott asked.

"Unclear. They also attempted to prevent our landing in Grand Prairie."

"So they're in the naval system?"

"Perhaps, or it could be they hacked into a single weather station. At this point we don't know. I had a message from the director twenty minutes ago. Other teams have been deployed to key points across the nation."

"Overreach by the national government to take charge of our operation," Quinn argued. "There's no indication that this attack has expanded to other Texas urban centers, let alone national ones."

"You mean other than sabotaging two planes of federal agents?" When Quinn didn't answer, Nora directed her final comment to Abbott. "We'll let you know if and when the federal situation changes."

Randall almost laughed at the expression on Quinn's face. He looked like a prize rooster that had been kicked out of the hen house. Randall had seen it before—locals convinced they didn't need help from the outside. But this attack was too big, too sophisticated, to worry about turf. Plus he'd seen tougher men and women than Quinn try to go up against Nora. He wanted to tell the guy to save his energy, because when it came to national security, she wasn't going to let anyone stand in their way.

℘

Chapter Three

Nora knew that Quinn saw her as the adversary, which didn't bother her at all. He could cooperate and stay on the operation, or fight them and be removed.

He'd been sitting in one of the desk chairs. Now he stood and smoothed his tie. If he stood any straighter, he could be an advertisement for back braces. "My people are one hundred percent certain..."

"Nothing's one hundred percent certain." The words popped out of Nora's mouth unbidden, but she felt no need to take them back. If Quinn really had that level of confidence, he was a fool. Or perhaps he simply hadn't seen the things she'd seen.

"We are certain..." Quinn pegged her with a look, then turned back toward the governor. "Other than the transportation issues Agent Brooks reported, we have no indication that the infection has spread beyond the DFW area."

"Good." Shelly's head bobbed up and down. "And what is the status here at this point?"

Quinn nodded to a rotund woman with reader glasses perched on the end of her nose. "Victoria

Johnson can answer that."

"Still cycling up," she said. "Degree of degradation increases by approximately 5.25% every hour."

"At this rate, we'll have a complete halt in transportation, utilities, communication, and infrastructure by midnight tonight."

"Have medical facilities been compromised?" Abbott asked.

An older man raised his hand. He had white hair pulled back in a ponytail, a close-cropped beard, and age spots on his hand. "Approximately thirty percent of our medical structure uses smart technology."

"And you are?"

"Travis Collins, sir. I've spoken with presidents of all major hospitals—including Parkland, Baylor, and Methodist Central. They'll postpone any surgeries that can be, pull in extra staff, and fall back on power outage procedures."

It seemed to Randall that Abbott visibly relaxed.

"Military facilities?" Nora asked.

It was Shelley who responded. "We only have reserve bases in the DFW area. They're on lock-down, technically speaking. Fort Hood, which is two hours to the south, is on high alert."

"All right." Abbott tapped the arm of his wheelchair. "I have an idea of how to brief the press then. If there's nothing else—"

"Actually there is."

Randall was watching the room rather than looking directly at his partner. He saw a couple of gazes sent heavenward—which wasn't so odd. No one appreciated feds coming in to fix local problems. He also saw at least two people whose expression passed closer to anger. What was that about? And what, if anything, should he do about it?

§

Nora stood, hands clasped behind her back, feet planted eighteen inches apart. "Randall has been analyzing the infected code. He's certain that the four-pronged attack is from four different perpetrators."

Quinn was back on his feet in seconds. "We've seen nothing to indicate that."

"Let her finish." Abbott's voice was soft, but brokered no argument.

"The signature is different for the infected code in each sector. He can forward what he has to your people, but there's no doubt about it. We're dealing with four different perpetrators, who, for whatever reason, have decided to coordinate their attack."

Groans broke out around the room.

"They're probably in four different locations."

"We might be able to trace the signature of one in time, but four?"

"Why would they do such a thing? Why no ransom?"

Nora pointed to Victoria Johnson. "That's the question we need to answer. If we can ascertain what they want, we're significantly closer to figuring out who they are."

Governor Abbott had a news conference scheduled immediately after the meeting. He thanked everyone for their efforts and wheeled away from the group, Shelly following closely behind him and then the rest of the group trailing like a group of ducklings.

Quinn barked at his people, then made his way over to Nora. "I'm sorry if I seemed a bit brusque."

"I don't care."

"Excuse me?"

"I don't care if you're brusque, Quinn. I don't care if your feathers are ruffled or your feelings are hurt. What I do care about is whether you're doing your job. As long as you are, we won't have a problem."

She half expected him to storm away, but instead he laughed. She wished she didn't have to deal with people like Quinn, but she did, so she folded her arms and waited.

"I think I'm going to like working with you, Brooks."

She waited, her expression hopefully neutral.

"I know. You don't care if I like you." Laughing again, he turned and walked away.

ℒ

Nora stared out the window, a cold cup of coffee in her hands. Though it was now midmorning, traffic was light on the streets of downtown Dallas. Abbott's speech had been well received, though some alternate news sites were already calling it a conspiracy to expand power on the state level. By and large, most people didn't mind a day off, and Abbott had assured them that the best minds in the country were working on the problem.

She glanced over at Randall.

He was locked into whatever was on his screen. She didn't doubt for a minute that he was the best. She'd asked to see his folder when the director had first told her that she had a new partner.

A new partner.

There were nights she still dreamed about what had happened in Shipshewana—receiving the call, seeing Tate's lifeless body, blaming herself for not being there.

In the end she'd caught the perp, who was now behind bars for life—well, she and an Amish farmer had caught him. She smiled at the thought of Benjamin Lapp. What would he think of their current situation? Had he ever been in a high rise office building? She doubted it. Nora suspected he was somewhere working in the sunshine, milking cows, and planting corn. It was a life she couldn't imagine, but one that appealed to her on some days.

She'd known that replacing Tate wouldn't be easy. No, replacing Tate would be impossible. There were still days she expected to see him walking around the corner of the office holding up a paper bag and grinning. "Sugar cinnamon. You know you want it." Everyone thought Nora had great intuition, and maybe she did—but Tate had taught her how to harness that intuition.

Randall was more like a young pup—full of energy and cockiness and potential. His IQ was a solid 124, a good 6 points above Nora's. He would be an asset to the agency in a few years. Truthfully, he was an asset now, but an untrained and untested one. As if sensing that she was watching, he glanced up, attempted a smile, then rubbed his eyes and returned his attention to the screen.

She turned and scanned the room. Quinn was meeting with ponytail guy. Travis Collins struck Nora as an unusual guy. People his age usually didn't have a handle on the scope of cyber risks and security. She wondered what his background was. The two men were bent over a print-out. Quinn seemed to trust him, so she supposed she'd have to as well.

The large woman, Victoria Johnson, was pacing back and forth as she stared at a handheld device. Another twenty agents were scattered around the room. They were all working, all tired, all focused. Only the three new people Abbott had assigned to them looked fresh. They'd set up their workstations in a little cluster in the southeast portion of the floor. As she watched, one tapped another on the shoulder and pointed to his screen.

She'd introduced herself when they first arrived, but now the clock had ticked toward eleven in the morning. Time to see what they knew. Two women and one man—all in their mid-twenties, dressed in jeans and t-shirts. They could have been three college kids meeting for a study group. They had millennial names to match their dress and attitude—Arya, Brynlee, and Cash.

Nora thought of Tate again, walked to the back of the room, and assembled a plate of donuts along with a few containers of yogurt and three bottles of water.

"How's it going?"

Cash looked up, seemingly surprised that his group wasn't the only one in the room. Then he noticed the plate of food and smiled. Snagged two donuts and a bottle of water. "Good."

"He thinks he found something," Brynlee explained, her hand hovering over the donuts but settling on the yogurt.

"We were about to take it to Quinn." Arya pulled her long hair back behind her shoulders, then pushed up her glasses.

"How about you show me first, and we'll decide together whether to bother Quinn with it."

Cash looked uncertain, but Arya reminded him, "She's the one from the agency. Federal trumps state."

"Indeed it does, and my name is Nora."

"Got it, Nora." Cash stuffed the last half of a donut into his mouth, brushed his fingertips against his jeans, then focused on his computer. "Everyone else is zoning in on the infected code, so I had the idea to look at what wasn't infected—what's being left for last and where there's a discernible reason why. Think about it. This is a targeted, structured attack. So what was their plan, their logic for doing it the way they're doing it?"

"And what were you able to ascertain?"

"Not much, at first, which is why I've been working on it for three hours with absolutely zero progress." His fingers flew over his keyboard, opening windows, lining them up sequentially, zooming in on certain portions. "There was progress. I just didn't realize it until Brynlee ran a repetitive pattern analysis."

"English, Cash." Nora suspected the kid was on to something, but she needed to be able to understand it. "Talk to me as if I'm a baby-boomer, which I'm not."

He glanced at Arya and Brynlee, who both nodded. "An address. We found an address."

"Show me."

Five minutes later, she walked away from the group. Quinn was watching her, but she acted like she didn't notice. She'd instructed Cash and Arya and Brynlee to keep the information within their group—

only share it with the governor and only if she wasn't back in an hour. That might be paranoia asserting itself, but better to play it safe. It didn't take more than two people to check out an address, unless their perp was there, and she highly doubted that.

She walked over to Randall. "Come with me."

He glanced up at her in surprise, but didn't ask any questions. Maybe he was learning.

They'd made it to the elevators before Quinn intercepted them.

"You've got something."

"We have a possible lead. We'll let you know if it pans out."

The elevator opened. Nora and Randall stepped on it.

"I'm still in charge of this command center. You have a duty to report to me any finds—"

"We'll let you know if it pans out." The door closed before he could come up with an assertive, somewhat angry, rebuttal.

"Intense guy."

"It's his turf. I get it."

"But you don't trust him."

Nora arched her back, felt the satisfying pop. "Let's get you some real coffee."

"Thought everyone stayed home from work today."

"Nope. Abbott left one Starbucks open—opiate of the masses and all that. I know where it is."

She explained to the guard outside the building where they needed to go. He pointed to the next crossroads. "Take a left at the light, and you'll see it on the right."

The Starbucks was full of people. Nora and Randall waited in line rather than push their way to the front. It felt good to be out of the stuffy room and away from the exhausted faces. The people surrounding them were full of energy, even if some of that was nervous energy.

The lights were off, though plenty of sunshine poured in through the windows. The heady smell of roasted coffee beans filled the room. A handwritten sign read, No microwaved items available.

Randall bumped Nora's shoulder with his. "How does this place have any power?"

"Generator. Every Starbucks has one."

"Seriously?"

"Hey. People need their coffee."

"Roads are closed." Randall glanced behind him as they shuffled forward. "How did these people get here?"

"They live here."

A couple in front of them turned around. The woman said, "We live next door, in the condos. Do you know anything about what's going on?"

"Nothing that we can share."

"Fair enough." The man shrugged. "I'm not arguing with a day off, and since the net is down I can't even work from home. Ha, ha. Joke's on the boss."

Nora waited until the couple had moved forward to continue the conversation with Randall. "Abbott's plan to isolate each municipality—technologically speaking—is a pretty good one, but I'm surprised he thought of it."

"Because he's not a techie?" Randall asked.

"Because he'd old. Most people his age don't

realize the scope and breadth of the web."

"It's true. They aren't even aware of the Internet of Things, though it's infiltrated every part of their life."

"I haven't heard that term in a while." Nora pointed at a bran muffin to the worker and asked for a coffee with two shots.

The man behind them shrugged his shoulders when Nora turned and scowled at him. "Sorry. Hard not to hear a conversation when we're crammed in this tight."

Everyone waiting in line was talking about the cyberattack. Nora wasn't worried about what he'd overheard. In fact, it might be good to get a fresh perspective. "What do you know about IoT?"

"It was freaking people out—the term. Internet of Things sounds like a Shyamalan movie." The man asked for a chocolate croissant and coffee with a shot.

"Sixth Sense," Randall said.

"Wayward Pines." Nora had enjoyed that one, though it wasn't as good as the book. Movies never were, in her opinion. "Do you work in IT?"

"I do. Nearly everyone here does in one way or another, though it won't appear on every job description. It's simply woven into our society now."

"Which is part of the problem," Nora muttered.

"When tech people started talking about the Internet of Things, non-tech folks started envisioning the machines rising up and taking over. Orwellian connotations were too strong, so there was like this tacit agreement to switch to IoT. Use an acronym and people's eyes pretty much glaze over."

"The man has a point." Randall reached for his wallet, but Nora stayed his hand.

Since they weren't able to take credit payments, everyone was paying with cash. She paid the cashier, dropped a couple bucks in the tip jar, and stuffed the receipt into her pocket.

"Have a good day," the man behind them said, as if they were all out for a morning's stroll.

"Yeah, you too." She snagged a table outside. The temperature was hovering in the 50s, but the sun was out and the fresh air was helping to clear her head. Once they'd sat down and dug into their food, she leaned closer to Randall, lowered her voice, and explained what Abbott's team had found.

"Why are we wasting time with coffee and muffins?"

"Because we need it, because if your brain isn't clear when you go into this, you're likely to miss something—and missing something can cost lives."

"Uh-huh. What else?"

Her satellite phone beeped. She pulled it out and stared down at the screen. "Brynlee was still chasing a few leads."

"And?"

"And we have an exact address now. Let's go."

ᔕ

Chapter Four

Nora was right about the coffee and croissants. They gave Randall a renewed burst of energy. By the time they'd walked back to the building that housed their makeshift headquarters, an unmarked car was waiting for them.

Fortunately, a local police officer was driving.

Everyone introduced themselves, and then Officer Fleming accelerated away from the curb. "Your address is less than ten miles. Even with the traffic lights out, I can have you there in fifteen minutes."

The fact that very few cars were out helped as well. They passed a Dallas Area Rapid Transit depot with DART buses lined up at the curb. With no traffic signals and no way to call 9-1-1 in the case of accidents, the transit authority had bowed to Abbott's call to cease all non-essential transportation. It wasn't worth the liability to put their drivers on the road.

They travelled north toward Highland Park, then turned east to Lower Greenville.

Fleming shifted in her seat. She was black, probably forty years old, and by the looks of it, a seasoned officer. "This area is in a real state of transition. You have half a million dollar condos across the street from public housing."

"How does that work?" Randall was riding in the back seat. He tapped his window, which looked out over a row of two-story brick apartments that had been built at least fifty years ago. Trash littered yards and not a single blade of grass or shrub threatened the place. People sat out on their stoop, smoking cigarettes or holding babies. Children from toddlers to teens gathered between the buildings playing ball or hopscotch or whatever kids played when their cell phones weren't working.

"Not very well, to tell you the truth. The lower class is getting pushed out due to urban revitalization." Her voice put quotation marks around the last two words. "While it's a boon for the real estate market, the people at the bottom have fewer and fewer places to go."

She made three more turns and arrived in front of a house that looked no better than the apartments they'd passed. "This area sits right in the middle of the turn war."

"War is a rather harsh term." Nora's hand was on the door handle, but she waited for the officer's reply.

"To you, it might. To the people living in these houses? They'll get bought out at bottom dollar, and then they'll have a tough time finding someplace else to live." Fleming nodded toward the house. "Want me to go in with you?"

"That won't be necessary. What we find will determine how long we'll be. I'll let you know."

Randall jogged to catch up with Nora. Apparently the caffeine had energized Nora as well. Had she had a double shot of espresso or a triple?

They did a perimeter sweep and met back at the front door. Randall checked the door frame for any signs of an explosive device, then nodded at Nora, who knocked loudly.

No answer.

Of course there wasn't. It couldn't be that easy.

"Want me to jimmy the lock?"

"Not necessary." She'd put her hand down into the bottom of the old mailbox attached next to the front door and pulled out a key.

"I didn't realize postal workers actually came to the door anymore."

"Only in old neighborhoods like this—another reason the city would like to see them bulldozed."

"No mail."

"There's a post office box associated with the address. Cash was able to get that far into the postal computers before the system crashed."

Randall pulled in a deep breath as Nora unlocked the door and they stepped into the place. He liked being out from behind a desk, but times like this—times there could be a bomb attached to the door or a guy with a gun sitting inside—he wondered if he was crazy for choosing field work.

Then they stepped into the room, and any thoughts of desk work evaporated like raindrops in the sun.

He let out a long, low whistle as they walked around the room, then into the kitchen and the single bedroom. Every room was the same, packed from floor to ceiling with boxes of what looked like unopened merchandise.

Only that wasn't quite right. He picked up a box holding a first generation iPad and studied it. Definitely it had been opened, then placed back inside exactly as it had been packaged.

Nora stopped in the middle of the living room, hands on her hips. "A hoarder? Our hacker is a hoarder? How does that make sense?"

"It kind of does." Randall squatted down in front of a tower of cellular phone boxes. "Though *collector* might be a better word than *hoarder*."

"Explain it to me."

"Hoarders often can't articulate why they keep something. They have an obsessive compulsive disorder to prepare for the future—any future. I knew a woman once who kept toothbrushes, printer paper, and green beans." He glanced up at Nora, a smile playing on his lips. "You couldn't walk through her house, and she couldn't explain to you why she had to buy yet another toothbrush when she saw one."

"Huh."

"This is different. This is...more like a very well-thought-out plan."

"For what? This stuff is all...old."

"That's exactly it." Randall hurried from the room, checking to see if what he thought was happening here, was in fact happening. When he returned to the living room, Nora was coming in from outside.

"I told Fleming we should be ready to go in a few minutes. This looks like a dead end."

"But it's not. Call Quinn and have him send a team over."

"A team?"

"They need to check for fingerprints, though I

suspect our guy—or gal—wore gloves."

"You think this is legit? That our cyberbug lives here?"

"I wouldn't say he or she lives here, but whoever it is definitely uses this place as a staging area." He tapped a tower of smart speakers. "These are all Gen 2 devices—not Gen 1."

"You lost me."

"Gen 1 was analog. Gen 2 was digital."

Nora walked over to him, put her hands on his shoulders and attempted to shake him.

He couldn't help laughing.

"Explain it in English."

"Okay. Look. Gen 1 was the first wireless technology, but it required a modem. Gen 2 was truly wireless. These devices stacked throughout this house... all of them...are Gen 2. They're not older and they're not newer."

"Why is that significant?"

"Because there are no security patches for Gen 2. Whoever is in charge of our cyberattack is using this house to send signals through."

"Someone could do that?"

"Sure. It's like this place is a giant amplifier to a part of the web that everyone thinks has been shut down."

"But it hasn't been."

"Not yet. They're working on it, to make room for 5G."

"You're making my head hurt."

"My point is that he's patching his code through these devices." He picked up a box that claimed to hold a baby cam set inside a wooly lamb. "He's hacking these machines, because they have no security patch. That's how he gets in...from there, the IoT can take care of the rest."

"The machines talk to each other."

"Exactly. It would be like getting a call on your cell phone from your great grandparent talking on a wall phone that has a long curly cord. You'd still be able to hear and understand grandpa."

"So if we turned off all these...devices, would that shut our perp down?"

"No. He—or she—is already in."

"So what do we do?"

"What we always do. We follow the trail." He had that fluttery feeling that he got when he was close. He could almost see how this had come together, but there were a few pieces missing.

"Back to headquarters?"

"Yeah, and I think we better hurry."

Nora didn't spend too long trying to understand what Randall had described. She had a basic understanding of the web—certainly more than most people—but less than an average computer geek. She didn't need to understand the intricacies of cyberbugs any more than she needed to understand the details of bomb makers. Her job was to catch the perp before he caused massive damage to people or systems.

He or *she*...

Nora glanced over at Randall and bit back a smile. He was learning to think outside the box, to put his preconceived notions aside and analyze what was in front of him. If she could teach him that, they'd make a great team. Randall understood aspects of the web and coding that sounded like foreign language to her. All that talk about Gen 1 and Gen 2 made her antsy. Generation X she could understand—baby boomer, millennial, even Gen Z. She understood people, especially the ones she was pursuing.

She'd been with the agency for ten years now. She could count on one hand the motives for cyber terrorism—greed, revenge, insanity, and warnings about the dangers of technology. She didn't even need her entire hand to count motives. No one planted a virus into a system because of unrequited love. She'd encountered only those four motives, and she didn't think for a moment that a new motive had sprouted out of the Texas dirt.

Sometimes if she could tag the motive, she could more easily find the perp. This was big. Whoever was doing this probably wasn't insane. It felt too well planned for that. Which left greed, revenge or warnings.

The last one bothered her the most. Those people couldn't be reasoned with. They were certain of their superiority—they were the only ones who truly understood the dangers facing not just America but civilization. They were convinced that the only way to avoid the collapse they so clearly foresaw was to bring the system—the entire system—down immediately.

Was that what they were dealing with now?

She wasn't sure.

Fleming took a different route back to their headquarters—over to I-75, then south to the Woodall Rogers Freeway, which gave them an excellent view of downtown Dallas. The place was eerily vacant, as were the roads. Whoever was behind this cyberattack had managed to bring the 9th most populous city in the United States to its knees.

To what end?

What were they hoping to achieve?

Fleming was exiting toward downtown when Nora's satellite phone rang. Randall glanced up from the tablet he'd been staring at. They rarely gave out the number to their SAT phones. Only the director, Governor Abbott, and Quinn had Nora's number—and of course Randall.

"Brooks."

"He wants to meet you." There was something in Quinn's voice she couldn't identify—a warning, or something he wasn't saying.

"Who?"

"Our perp. He hired a courier—some kid we're holding. The message says to meet him at two p.m. at the Fountain Place."

"Hold." Nora covered the mouth piece, pulled the phone away from her ear and addressed Fleming. "Change of plans. Can you take us to Fountain Place?"

"Sure thing."

She put the phone back to her ear. "We're on our way."

"I have the Chief of Police on hold, waiting your instructions."

Nora glanced at Randall.

Should they go in alone? Or would they need the back-up?

As if reading her mind, Randall shrugged.

She spoke back into the phone. "Three men, plain clothes, tell them to meet us..."

Randall had pulled up a map of downtown Dallas on his tablet. "Meet us at the corner of Ross and Freeman."

"Anything else?"

Nora couldn't tell if he was being sarcastic or truly wanted to help. She'd have to hope for the latter.

"Send a photo of the message to my phone."

She clicked off and turned to her partner.

"Think it's real?" he asked.

"Nope."

"Feels too early for a show-down."

"It does."

"But it's something."

"Could be a decoy. Could be a trap."

"Cheer up, Nora. Maybe it's just another clue." Randall tapped his fingers against the edge of the tablet. "Maybe he's messing with us to see if we're as smart as we think we are."

"Are we?"

"Time will tell."

Fleming met their gaze in the rearview mirror. "You two sure take this stuff in stride."

Now it was Nora's turn to shrug. She turned her gaze out the window. "It's not the end of the world, Officer Fleming."

"Feels like it when everything stops working."

"And that is their goal. If you feel trapped, you'll bend."

Fleming pulled to a stop at the corner of Ross and Freeman. "Should I wait?"

"No. We'll catch a ride back with the police chief. Be safe." Nora slammed the door without waiting for an answer.

As the officer's car pulled away, Randall stood beside her, reading from his tablet as she gazed up at the glass tower. "Forty-two floors, design is a multi-faceted prism, completed in 1986, and named after 172 fountains."

"Great. Mirrors, angles, and water."

"Our perp is definitely playing with us."

"It would seem." Her phone binged, and she opened the attachment from Quinn.

> You have one chance to end this.
> Fountain Place. Mezzanine level.
> Brooks and Goodwin only.
> 2:00.

Nora frowned at the screen. "Why the mezzanine level?"

"Why here?"

"How did they know our names?"

"And why do they want to negotiate with us?"

Nora crammed the phone back into her jacket pocket. "I'm pretty sure this is not a negotiation."

They hurried over to the two men and a woman who stood twenty yards back from the intersection. Each person stepped forward, shook hands, and introduced their self.

"Police Chief, Keith Sowars."

"Assistant Chief, Mitzi Nguyen."

"Captain, James Wright."

Nora and Randall introduced themselves, then quickly briefed the Dallas group on what they thought was happening.

"I might know a good place to survey the

situation." Wright glanced at his bosses, who both nodded for him to continue. "The front of the building, in the middle the fountain area. Lots of trees—and they're live oaks so they'll still have their leaves. Should provide plenty of cover."

"Let's do it."

As they jogged toward the front of the building, Nora glanced at her watch. They had fourteen minutes to decide how they were going to handle this.

No water came out of the fountains. The pumps had stopped when the electricity cut out. The place wasn't completely deserted, though. There were at least a dozen teenagers on skateboards enjoying their day off.

"I'll clear the area." Nguyen turned toward the teens, but Nora stopped the woman with a hand on her arm. "Wait. We might need them."

Nguyen cocked her head to the side, waiting to hear what reason Nora would have for endangering the lives of civilians—and not just civilians, but under-aged civilians.

Instead of explaining herself, Nora turned to Randall. "What do you think?"

He crossed his arms and shifted his weight from one foot to the other. "I don't like it. Something isn't... we're not seeing the full picture here."

"Agreed."

Nora turned to Sowars and Wright. "CCTV?"

Wright shook his head. "All the closed circuit televisions are currently disabled—per the governor's orders."

"So our perp isn't watching us right now."

"Unless he's inside," Sowars pointed out. "Not that he could see us from here, but he'll see you approach and enter the building."

"He's not here. I can guarantee you he's not in that building, so why does he want us in there on the mezzanine level?" Nora turned back to Randall, but he was already ahead of her. She didn't even have to ask the question.

"Even if he has hacked into one of the federal satellites, he can't track us via the car we were in or our civilian phones. They're both routed through commercial providers who are currently down. All the GPS feeds are down, but the satellite phones are a different matter."

Which again pointed to someone on the inside.

She'd figure that out later.

Instead of calling Quinn, she punched in the number for Abbott's millennial group.

Brynlee answered.

"Are the brown-outs still cycling?"

"Yup."

"I'm at 1445 Ross Ave. Tell me when it's scheduled to come back on here."

"If the pattern stays the same, it'll cycle back on at 1:57 and stay on for four minutes."

"Thanks."

Nora disconnected the call and strode toward the closest teenager, who performed a complicated skateboard maneuver that shot him up three steps then spun him in a half circle. Once he was facing her, he popped the board up and caught the end of it.

"Let me guess. We have to leave."

"Not exactly. I want to borrow your board."

"This board?" The kid looked fifteen, had the requisite long hair that had been carefully styled to look as if he hadn't combed it in a week, and was sporting a good case of acne.

Nora didn't miss being a teen.

But she remembered what it was like to be that age. You wanted to be the one making the decision, and you could usually use extra money.

"How much?" Nora reached for her wallet and pulled out five twenties.

"I paid double that."

Nora doubted it, but she didn't have time to haggle. She pulled a hundred more, made the exchange, and smiled when the kid said, "I should have asked for three."

"Tell your friends we need them off this block—now."

By the time she'd walked back to Randall, he'd already procured a roll of duct tape. Where had he found that? She didn't take the time to ask. Instead, they secured both of their SAT phones to the board.

"Four minutes." Randall nodded toward the building. "Want me to take it in?"

"Nope. This is why I get paid the big bucks. You're going to want to stand back from these fountains."

Nora took off at a jog, while Randall explained to the others what she was doing.

No one was visible in the building—no guards, no business people. She reached the door at exactly 1:57 as the electricity powered back on. Water surged through the fountains behind her, and the front door opened easily. Whoever was orchestrating this wanted her inside.

Ambient light had come on around the main lobby, and more importantly, the escalator she'd seen from outside had started operating, stretching from the lobby up to the mezzanine level. She popped the skateboard on the bottom step, made sure it was moving up, then took off at a jog.

She'd reached the edge of the fountain area when an explosion shook the building behind her. Glass rained down around her and sirens pierced the afternoon.

At least she knew why their perp wanted her and Randall on the mezzanine level. That was where he'd planted the bomb.

He wanted to kill them.

Chapter Five

Randall felt as if he had sand in his eyes and rubbing them only increased the gritty feeling. He leaned back in his chair, closed his eyes, and saw lines of code dancing along the inside of his eyelids.

Yup.

He needed sleep.

"How's the head?" Nora dropped into the chair beside him, holding a bottle of water in one hand and a steaming cup of coffee in the other.

Randall wanted the coffee.

He chose the water.

He needed to hydrate.

"This little scratch?" He raised his left forefinger to touch the butterfly stitch above his right eye. It was actually kind of cool if he ignored the fact that he might have been killed. Flying glass was nothing to laugh at. Neither was almost getting blown up. But his first on-the-job injury? Now that would be a great story to tell once he got back home.

If he got back home.

"You're a tough guy. You know it?"

Randall rolled his eyes. "Now you're mocking me."

Nora had been thrown by the power of the blast. She had four stitches in her left shoulder and a nice-sized scratch under her right eye and would probably be sporting a shiner by morning.

"Not at all. Butterfly stitches look nice on a guy your size." She picked up a pen and twirled it through her fingers, staring out the window.

Sunset had occurred hours ago. A light rain shower had pushed through around seven o'clock. The same people who'd been in the command center when they arrived were still there. Even Governor Abbott had returned.

Rumor was that he'd received two calls from the president.

"Did you talk to the director?"

"I did."

"And?"

"And the good news is that there's no indication this is happening anywhere except here."

"You call that good news?"

"Could be a prototype attack. Or could be the perp has something against Dallas."

"Or is from Dallas."

"Exactly."

"What motive are you leaning toward?" He was well aware of her theory of four motives.

"Greed's out."

"Unless someone is paying him...or her."

"Doesn't feel like insanity."

"Too methodical."

"Which leaves revenge..."

"Or warnings." He picked up a squeeze ball and tossed it from his right hand to his left and back again.

Right to left and back.

Right to left and back.

Suddenly he sat up straighter, pulled his keyboard toward himself, and pulled up four different windows. He studied them a minute, then turned to Nora. "Warnings fits best. This perp is making a point with the Gen 2 devices."

"He's worried about the 5G network?"

"Exactly."

"What are the dangers of 5G?"

"Some experts are worried about radiation. We could be dealing with someone who's had a family member die of cancer."

"What else will 5G do?"

"It opens the way for self-driving cars."

"All right. Our perp could be someone who's loved one has died in a car wreck...autonomous or otherwise. What else?"

"Global grid."

"And conspiracy theories."

Randall leaned back in his chair. "Some people say we're not merely building a faster global network. They say we're building a global microwave oven."

"So our perp is making a point by bringing the system down."

"Showing what they can do by bringing down one major metropolitan area."

"In which case we'd expect an if/then scenario. If world leaders agree to halt advancement on the 5G grid, then..."

"Then they'd let the 4G grid stand. A cold war

mentality. Détente in the cyber age."

Nora stood, put her hands at the bottom of her back, and stretched.

"Still seeing that chiropractor guy?"

"I am, though there doesn't seem to be one in this room." She checked her watch. "We've got two hours."

"And then what?"

"No one knows, but I'm guessing we'll find out. Keep working on the Gen 2 angle. I'm going to go snoop around."

Randall refocused on the data in front of him.

The answer was there, in the house they'd visited.

An icon appeared at the bottom of his screen.

New Message
Sender: Arya
Your Eyes Only

Randall glanced around, then opened the file. It was a listing of the devices that had been catalogued from the house. As he'd suspected, every item was Gen 2. One-third of the items still had a functional battery in them. All had been remotely accessed at some point in the last seven days.

Seven days.

So the event didn't start forty-eight hours ago. That was only when they'd become aware of it. The event, whatever it was, had actually begun when those devices were accessed. It had been cycling up for a week.

He knew when the gadgets were accessed.

But when were they purchased?

He replied to the message, asking Arya to get him the data.

Glancing up, he saw Nora sitting with Victoria, the large woman who worked for Quinn. She was fiddling with her reader glasses and glancing around as if she expected someone to jump out and yell BOO.

He didn't know what that was about.

Then his computer binged again.

Another note from Arya.

Again marked Your Eyes Only. How was she even sending these? They weren't coming over Quinn's network. She was bouncing them off a remote satellite.

Why?

What was she trying to tell him?

Who didn't she trust? Nora was convinced someone in this room was working with the terrorist, and apparently Arya and her group shared the same opinion.

Randall checked to make sure no one was close enough to read his screen, then clicked on the new message.

He leaned closer, confirming the data, the dates, and the corresponding news article. Another piece of the puzzle had fallen into place.

༄

Nora stared at Victoria. Every cell in her body wanted to turn around and scan the room for Quinn. She'd entered what she'd come to think of as the center of a cyber storm. In her mind it was akin to the eye of a hurricane. Everything depended on how she reacted now.

It had been a few minutes past ten when she was speaking with Randall. She'd gone to the restroom, stopped by Cash's station, and then ended up at Victoria's.

"You're absolutely certain about this?"

"Sure. Don't take my word for it though. You can easily do a web search for the details. Wait. Maybe you can't..."

"Did you notice any change in Quinn, after the accident?"

"He was back in the office faster than anyone expected, acting as if everything was business as usual."

"But it wasn't."

"Look." Victoria put her glasses on, then snatched them off again. "He's my boss, and I'm not making any accusations. Okay? I want to be clear on that. I need this job."

"Noted."

"You asked me if anyone had experienced a family tragedy in the last few years. As far as I know, Quinn's the only one who has."

"And you've been here a long time?"

Victoria glanced over at Arya and Brynlee and Cash. "Since those three were in diapers."

"Got it." Nora stood, tried to appear casual as she made a circuit of the room. Her stomach clenched and she felt as if she couldn't draw in a full breath.

Maybe he was in the bathroom.

Maybe he'd stepped outside to get some fresh air.

Ten-thirty. Ninety minutes until the system around the Dallas area completely crashed. Quinn wasn't outside or grabbing some chow.

He was gone.

She hurried to Randall's station, leaned down, and whispered. His eyes widened in surprise, but he didn't say a word. Instead he nodded once and turned back to his keyboard.

Nora headed to the elevators.

Sixty seconds later on the dot, Randall joined her.

He started to ask a question, but she shook her head.

Once the elevator doors had closed, she told him what she'd learned. "Quinn's divorced. His daughter was killed when her mom was driving her to the mall. They were hit by a self-driving car. The company settled out of court for 3.2 million."

"Let me guess. It happened three years ago."

"How did you know that?"

"It's when our perp started buying Gen 2 devices, and it's also when legislation passed opening up a large section of the 5G grid to automated vehicles."

The elevator deposited them on the ground floor. Nora no longer cared if anyone was watching. They had to stop Quinn before he did the thing he was planning to do—the thing he'd been planning from the beginning. She was certain his goal wasn't simply to temporarily halt any production or communication. Revenge and warnings were both powerful motives—combined, it meant he had something big in mind. Something that would catch the entire world's attention.

৯৹

"Where are we headed?" Randall jogged to catch up with Nora. His watch said two minutes after eleven. Whatever was going to happen, they had fifty-eight minutes to stop. Why were they running through downtown Dallas? Certainly, a car—any car—would be faster.

Nora passed the JFK memorial, then stopped at the intersection of Main and South Houston. She was in amazing shape for a woman her age.

Who was he kidding?

She wasn't even eleven years older than he was. He needed to exercise more.

He leaned over, hands on knees, and told her what Arya had sent him—the dates of the purchases had begun on the anniversary of the death of Quinn's daughter over five years earlier.

"And that very same anniversary is tomorrow..."

"In fifty-two minutes."

As they continued walking, Nora told him what Victoria had said about the car accident and the settlement.

"So Quinn's rich?"

"He's divorced and childless."

"Yeah, that too."

The shower that had passed through earlier that evening left the pavement wet. The blinking traffic lights combined with the total lack of vehicles or pedestrians paid homage to the fact that all was not well. No one knew exactly what was going to happen, what the *Midnight Strike*, as Abbott had so aptly called it, would entail. Apparently the great majority of the population had decided to face the crisis from their homes. Randall was grateful for that at least.

"What are we looking at?"

"Texas Book Depository—where Oswald shot Kennedy from—is over there."

"And you think that's where Quinn went?"

"No. I don't." She turned in a circle. "Too obvious, not flashy enough."

"Grassy knoll is that way?"

"Yes, but he's not sitting on the side of the road with his laptop. No, he'd want to be protected. He'd want to be..." she scanned the skyline, the silhouettes of the skyscrapers barely visible with the power cut. Abbott had been adamant—traffic lights at main intersections, hospitals, police and fire stations. What was left of the juice in the grid would only go to those locations. The buildings that housed the movers and shakers of the Dallas scene...they stood dark against the night sky.

"He'd want to be above it all." She turned in a circle once more, then pointed to the south. "Reunion Tower."

She took off again, Randall matching her pace this time. He definitely needed an exercise regime. He could be a jogger. He could take that up. Or maybe he needed to work out in the gym, pump a little iron.

They ran less than a mile, then stopped at the base of the building.

"How are we going to get in?"

But Abbott had thought of that too, or maybe he'd only thought of keeping people out. Regardless, there was a soldier stationed at the main entrance to the tower.

Nora flashed her credentials. "We're looking for a tall guy, nearly seven feet, thin and bald. He's probably carrying a laptop or a backpack."

"No, ma'am. No one's been here. The place is locked down."

"Is there a back entrance?"

"You'd have to have a special key, and as far as I

know the computer system is down, so you couldn't get in anyway."

"Quinn could. Quinn would've planned a way."

Nora started around the corner of the building.

Once again Randall jogged to catch up. "So you think Quinn is the mastermind? Not just part of a coordinated attack."

"He probably brought other people in. That's why you noted the four different signatures in the code."

"But he was the driving force, the one leaking information to the others."

"Makes sense. Doesn't it? He's been there from the beginning. He knew what was happening as it was happening. He's the only one who could have coordinated it."

"But why? How is this going to bring his daughter back?"

Nora glanced at him. "We never know why. Not really."

The employee entrance at the back of the tower had a keypad that had been busted. The glass door had been shattered. Nora's footsteps made a crunching sound as she ground the glass to pieces. She nodded toward the elevator, which was going up.

"How did he..."

But Nora wasn't listening. She'd already started up the stairs.

"Fifty-six flights? Tell me you're kidding."

"Eight hundred and seven steps according to the sign we passed. Better save your breath."

"And what if we're chasing some kids who dared each other to break into the tower?"

"Kids couldn't have activated the elevators. Only

Quinn could have done that."

She was right. The lack of oxygen must be affecting his brain. They passed the third floor mark, and he decided to shut up and focus on climbing the next fifty-three flights of stairs.

Nora stopped one floor shy of the top. They'd both been carrying pen lights, and hers was pointed to the floor as they rested on their haunches.

"Do you think he knows we're coming?" Randall hated the way his breath rattled around in his chest. When had he become old? Of course even the young Randall probably couldn't have sprinted up fifty flights of stairs. He should be proud he'd made it.

"I don't see how."

"No cameras or sensors in these stairwells?"

"He wouldn't have risked it. The elevators were a blip, he could hope to get away with it, but to actively monitor security cams would ping his own command center. He wouldn't risk that."

"Okay. So what's the point? Why is he here?"

Nora peered up at him, her expression grim and determined. "Because he wanted to see. He could have done this electronically, but he wanted a front row seat."

"And now?"

"Now he has a 360 degree view of his destruction."

"What destruction?"

Instead of offering a suggestion, she shrugged and stood, pulled her handgun, released the clip, checked that it was full, and slapped it back into the place. Randall did the same. "I'm going in first. Give me..." She studied her watch, motioned for him to make sure that his coordinated with hers. "We have twelve minutes. You give me seven, then come in."

"I'm not hiding in this staircase for seven minutes."

"Seven minutes. Not before. You come in behind me, but stay back where he won't see you."

"And what are you going to do?"

Nora stepped closer, put a hand on his arm, and met his gaze. "I'm going to try to stop him. If I fail, you do what you have to do, Randall. Do your job."

"I'm not sure what you're saying."

She pulled back the slide. Her right hand held the pistol and with her left she reached for the door knob. "You give me until five minutes before midnight—not a second longer."

᪉

Chapter Six

Nora pushed through the door and stepped into the Five Sixty restaurant. The open floor plan provided a panoramic view, and it didn't take long to spot the sole occupant.

Quinn sat at one of the tables offering a pristine observation point of the Dallas metroplex and beyond. All was dark—the few working traffic lights did little to pierce the darkness. One point four million people, without light, without power, waiting.

"I knew the minute you showed up in my command center that you were going to be trouble."

"And I thought you were one of the good guys."

"At first maybe you did, but you figured the truth pretty quickly."

She didn't bother denying it. She'd had her suspicions about him almost from the beginning. Cyberbugs didn't coordinate, not that well. It had to be someone on the inside, someone offering unprecedented access.

Quinn's right hand held a Glock pistol, pointed directly at her. At first Nora couldn't understand how she was able to see him, and then she realized that he'd hacked into the facility's lighting. He'd activated the ambient lighting only—enough to allow him to aim well, but not spoil his view of the darkened Dallas skyline.

His left hand rested on the keyboard of an open laptop, fingers poised and ready to hit the one key that would cause the cascade of destruction—assuming he could still do that, assuming they hadn't succeeded in thwarting his plan. The fact that he was here told Nora they hadn't been successful enough. There was something he was intent on completing, something he'd come here to do.

"Where's your sidekick?"

"Your guy got him. Old guy, long hair—he was yours, right?"

"I wasn't sure if Travis would have the wherewithal to see this through. He was a newer recruit."

"You planned this carefully." She was inching slowly closer, praying that Randall was remaining down and out of sight, that he'd follow orders and not try to be a hero. Actually, she needed him to be a hero, just not yet. If things went south, and something told her they might, she needed him to pick up the pieces.

"You're wasting your time, Agent Brooks."

"How's that?"

"You're not going to distract me by appealing to my sense of pride."

"I wasn't aware that was what I was doing." She nodded toward his laptop. She was now close enough to read the digital countdown that dominated his screen. "We have ten minutes. Might as well talk about something."

"If you shoot me, you still won't be able to stop the program."

"Can't blame me for trying."

"If I shoot you, I'll still be here to watch the cumulative differential of my work."

She slid into the booth across from him, placed the Sig Sauer on the table, then dropped her hands into her lap. Her backup piece was strapped to her ankle. Shooting him wouldn't work, though. Nora wanted answers. "So let's watch it together."

"I don't believe you. You're not the type to give up."

"Whose giving up? I just climbed fifty-six flights of stairs. Takes a lot out of a person."

"You're tenacious. I'll give you that." His eyes danced with adrenaline...and perhaps something else. Perhaps he'd needed a little chemical assistance to see this through. Or it could be the fire and passion and certainty of the touched, the only one who understood, the person who was going to set the world straight. And Quinn understood firsthand the cost of technology gone awry.

It was the true believers that Nora always feared most of all.

But it wasn't fear that Nora felt now. It was a calm acceptance. She would stop him, and if she had to give her life to do that, so be it.

Good people had died for far less.

Her mind flashed back to her previous partner, Tate, and his lifeless body in a small town called Shipshewana. There was no shame in giving your life for your country—for the families and the kids and the unborn who had a right to experience all that she had.

Her grandparents' house, her father's hand holding hers, her mom setting a plate of food down in front of her.

Ben Lapp explaining prayer over a home-cooked breakfast.

The way the stars had looked outside the C-20 Gulfstream. Nylah and Curtis and Randall. The director. Governor Abbott. All good people who would carry on, but only if she succeeded in stopping the madman across from her.

"Nine minutes, agent. What's your move?"

"Explain it to me, so I can appreciate it. You had four coders—yourself, Travis...who else?"

"Used two international sources. I could have done it myself, but I knew you'd be able to track a single coder faster. As things stand, the code is all in place and there's nothing you can do to stop it."

"What happens next?"

His grip tightened on the pistol, but his finger remained next to, not on, the trigger.

She thought he'd ignore her request, but who else did he have to talk to? And the geniuses always wanted to enlighten those beneath them.

"The grid is designed to come back online slowly. When I turn it on all at once—and yes I can override Abbott's supposed firewall—"

"The substations will explode—all of them at once."

"A series of explosions actually. It will be like dominoes falling one after the other." His voice softened, and he glanced toward the window. "It will be beautiful."

"Why?"

"Because it's bound to happen eventually. Better

to control the when and where and how."

"Fatalistic."

"No less true."

"Why is it bound to happen?"

"You know why." He leaned forward, his left hand still on the keyboard. The hand on the pistol raised slightly to make his point. "The Internet of Things—it's them or us. You should be thanking me."

"You're doing this for your daughter. You blame the IoT for her death."

"The IoT will do more damage than I ever could." He laughed—a hollow, mirthless sound. "Very good. You figured it all out."

She could no longer see the countdown clock, but she'd always had a good sense of time. Seven minutes until Quinn tapped the key that would activate the code. Two minutes until Randall made moved in. She watched for movement reflected in the glass windows behind Quinn. Randall would be coming from the side, aiming toward the windows. She needed both hands free to grab the laptop. She had to keep Quinn from using it as a shield.

"Your move, agent."

"I still don't have one. We both know that."

"You have a refreshingly honest way about you."

"There isn't really time for lies."

"We could have used you on our side."

"I would never be on your side."

Anger clouded his features, and then he reached for his Glock.

Every fiber in Nora's body screamed out for her to grab her Sig Sauer, put an end to the man sitting across from her, but she ignored that instinct.

Quinn palmed the Glock and flipped the safety off at the same moment that Nora caught Randall's reflection in the glass. She grabbed the laptop and dropped across the booth's seat with the laptop under her.

Time slowed.

Ben Lapp's words came back to her, almost as if he were whispering them in her ear.

No one is born believing.

We all have to work out our own faith, in our own way.

It might be a foxhole prayer, but she wasn't proud. The fact that she was desperate and scared didn't stop her. She prayed. She called out to God. She prayed they would stop this, that she hadn't activated any fail safe when she'd slapped the laptop's lid shut.

Four shots rang out.

She thought one was from Quinn, but she couldn't be sure and she didn't want to sit up until she knew it was safe to bring out the laptop. Wind whistled through the broken glass, and then Randall was there, pulling her up and taking the laptop from her.

She looked over at Quinn, or what was left of him. Randall's three shots had all found center of mass.

"He talked about the IoT."

"I heard him." Randall was sitting at the adjacent table, the laptop opened before him. His fingers flew over the keyboard. He hit a combination of keys. The countdown clock, now at three minutes, twenty-eight seconds minimized to the bottom of the screen. The screen itself was a stream of code.

Nora jumped to her feet, pulled out her new SAT phone to call the command center, then realized the phone wasn't showing a signal. Maybe it had been damaged in the fire fight. Or maybe Quinn had planned for that too.

She glanced out over the skyline—still dark, still waiting. There was nothing she could do but wait with them, wait on Randall, pray that he could crack the code, pray that they'd be given another chance. She wasn't sure how much she believed in divine intervention and God and foxhole prayers, but she prayed anyway. It mattered that much. There might not be anyone listening, but if there was...

"I've got it. At least, I think I've got it."

She rushed around to stand behind him. The clock read forty-two seconds until midnight, until the dominoes began to fall, until Quinn's destruction was set into motion.

Nora collapsed into the chair across from Randall. He looked up at her, his finger hovering over the enter key, his eyes asking if she was sure.

"Do it."

ᵔ

Two days later, they were standing in the jet bridge at DFW International Airport.

"There's not going to be any leg room on this plane." Randall moved forward, a frown firmly knotted between his eyes.

"Yup. We're just another cog in the wheel of domestic travel now."

"The C-20 was nice."

"Can't argue with that."

A child in front of them held up her doll to her

mother. "We're tired. We want you to carry us."

Dad picked her up instead. "Mom's holding Baby John. How about I carry you and Sasha?"

"Okay."

"Okay."

Randall met her gaze, and everything clicked together. She experienced that moment when the exhaustion fell away and the next case hadn't been set in motion yet and you knew that everything you'd endured had been worth it. Because they had succeeded, the family standing in front of them was having just another day, just another trip, and life would go on as if nothing had happened. Life would go on as it should.

"You never told me who the guy was."

"Guy?"

"The one you were having dinner with—in the fancy restaurant."

"Oh, that guy."

"It was a date. That much was obvious."

"Goodwin, did I say or do something to suggest I wanted to share my personal life with you?"

"We're partners."

"Uh-huh."

"We have each other's back."

She thought of the shots, reaching for the laptop, hovering in the booth. "Uh-huh."

"But if you don't want to talk about it."

"I don't."

"I'm not going to be able to stretch my legs out on this plane."

Randall's bantering melded into the sounds around her, and Nora allowed herself to relax for a brief moment. Then the pilot leaned out of the cockpit, looked down the row of passengers crossing from the jet bridge into the plane, and found her. He made the universal motion of holding a phone, then said something to the flight attendant, who motioned her past the others.

Nora stepped into the cockpit and accepted the phone as the pilot said, "It's someone called the director...said he needed to speak with you."

The End

Author's Note

This book is dedicated to my family, who tolerate my fascination with conspiracy theories and cyber warnings. My understanding of technological advances is less than complete; however, I am concerned about our growing dependence on technology both personally and globally. This series is designed to raise awareness regarding that dependence as well as any corresponding vulnerability. If the subject interests you, I suggest you do some research. In my opinion, knowledge is a good thing.

As is always the case, I am grateful for my pre-readers, Kristy and Tracy. This story was also made better by Teresa, who served as editor, cover designer, and formatter. All three of you are awesome.

And finally ...always giving thanks to God the Father for everything, in the name of our Lord Jesus Christ (Ephesians 5:20).

Blessings,
Vannetta

Daybreak

Cyber Division, Book 3

Dedicated to
Pam Lindman,
who loves a dystopian story
as much as I do.

While this novella is set against the real backdrop of Seattle, Washington, the characters as well as the community are fictional. There is no intended resemblance between the characters in this book and any real persons. As with any work of fiction, I've taken license in some areas of research as a means of creating the necessary circumstances for my characters. My research was thorough; however, it would be impossible to be completely accurate in details and descriptions. Therefore, any inaccuracies portrayed in this book are completely due to fictional license.

Contents

"To God belong wisdom and power;
counsel and understanding are his."
~Job 12:13

"The young people today are the 21st century."
~Martin Scorsese

❡

Chapter One

Nora Brooks and Randall Goodwin stepped out of Starbucks into a day fresh with the promise of spring. Seattle was showing off—the cherry trees were covered with pink and white blossoms, streets around the fish market were filled with people enjoying the sun-filled day, and the waters of Puget Sound glimmered in the distance.

"Tell me again why we're here."

Nora studied her stylishly dressed partner. She didn't know how he managed to look unrumpled after traveling across the country on the red-eye flight, but he did.

"Is that a Bottega jacket?"

"Very good. You've been paying attention to my fashion lessons, though..." He hesitated before adding, "Apparently it hasn't brought about any changes in your wardrobe."

Nora wore what she always wore—black pants, flat dress shoes that she could run in if the situation required, and a button-up cotton blouse. She tended to stick with white, gray, and sky blue.

There was no doubt in her mind that Randall's jacket cost more than everything she had on, including the diamond earring studs that was her only bow to sentimentality. Her parents had given her the earrings when she was promoted to her current position within the agency.

She popped the top off her drink and blew on the hot beverage—a tall, dark blend coffee, shot of espresso, whipped cream.

"Extra espresso?"

"Yup." She nodded toward the larger drink he was holding. "Caramel macchiato? I thought you were going to ease up on the sugar."

"I like caramel. That stuff you drink is like jet fuel."

Randall was six foot four with light brown skin and the physique of a professional football player. His father had enjoyed a long and prosperous NFL career, but Randall's love was computers, more specifically the code that made everything run and often caused the most chaos. At twenty-seven, he seemed like a babe to her. Nora had turned thirty-nine the week before. She was beginning to view everything through a cynical lens. Probably she needed a vacation.

"We're here to follow a hunch, and you're crabby because you spent last week in the Caribbean."

"I love the Caribbean."

"Coming back to work is never easy." She wiggled her eyebrows as she settled into a chair at one of the outdoor tables and took her first sip of the espresso. "Sure you're not ready to retire? Live off your dad's millions? With your coding skills, you could freelance from a cabana."

"And miss hanging out with you? Nah."

She was relieved to hear it. Randall was a good partner, and she didn't have the time to waste breaking in a new one.

"So we're following a hunch. How did you get the director to sign off on that?"

Nora shrugged. "All the other active cyber threats have been assigned."

"Unusual."

"Isn't that the truth." They'd had a solid schedule since the Dallas event. First a dam's controls had been hacked in the northeast, then ransom ware infiltrated CDC servers in Atlanta, and after that the electrical grid in Oklahoma City was compromised.

Nora had spent the week Randall was on vacation filling out paperwork for their past assignments. She'd jumped at the chance to get back out in the field.

"So what are we facing?"

"Unknown."

"Timeline?"

"Unknown."

"Perpetrator?"

She simply shook her head and gulped more of the coffee, grateful for caffeine. She had to give Randall credit. He didn't push. Instead he waited patiently as she decided how she wanted this op to unfold. Sometimes she held back information so Randall could assess a thing with fresh eyes. Sometimes he needed to know everything up front. Honestly, she only had one idea as to where to start, so she might as well level up with him now.

She pulled out her phone, opened a folder of pictures, and passed it to him.

"Miguel Garcia. Forty-two years old. Body found down by the wharfs by a couple of dock workers."

"Cause of death was apparently a shot to the head." Randall shook his head as he studied the photo. "We don't usually investigate homicides."

"Local detectives pulled his phone records. The last activity on his cell binged our department."

Randall looked up in surprise.

"He was tracing an IP address."

"That's not possible."

"It's not supposed to be. It's hard enough for law enforcement to convince a provider to hand over that information."

"Though a judge will order it in the case of a homicide."

"And that's exactly what happened. Only when Detective Lawson followed up on the information, it led to a Starbucks café."

"This one?"

"Yup."

"Doesn't answer the question of how Garcia had a program that could trace IP addresses."

"Or why he would want such a thing."

"Or who he was chasing." Randall handed the phone back to her.

"I'm a little surprised that single thing binged the director's program. Doesn't exactly sound like a cyber attack."

"Let's walk."

They strode down the street, passing vendors hawking flowers, jewelry, produce, and of course fish.

"What do you suspect?"

"That something's happening, and that it's big."

She didn't say anything else until they reached a view of Puget Sound. She'd been to Seattle several times, but never in April and never on a day as sunny and pure as the one before her. "Tell me what you see."

"Water. Islands in the distance. I think those are ferries farther out. And...cruise ships. Lots of cruise ships."

"Exactly. Seattle is a hub for Alaska and Pacific Northwest cruises. There are two cruise terminals. Pier 66 is eleven acres and home to Norwegian and Oceania Cruise Lines. Pier 91 is there to the north. It serves all the others—Carnival, Celebrity, Holland America, Princess, and Royal Caribbean."

"You thinking of becoming a tourist guide?"

"Those two terminals host eleven home port vessels. A total of 200 vessels dock here between May and October, providing service to over a million tourists a year."

"Huh." Randall finished his drink and tossed the cup into a nearby trashcan. "Looks like everyone is home this morning."

"And it's been that way for a week."

"Why?"

"That's where we start. We find out."

"And you think this is connected to Garcia's murder?"

"I don't believe in coincidences. We have a dead man who was tracing down an IP address with a program the government would drool to get its hands on, and an unexplained situation down on those ships that's affecting over a million people."

"We usually don't worry about cyber attacks on private business. They have their own people."

"No one is calling this is a cyber attack—yet."

"But you think it is."

"I think that something is off, and my spidey sense tells me it's cyber related."

"Because?"

"Because the cruise industry contributes 900 million a year to the Seattle economy."

"But only if the ships are running."

"Exactly."

"And the director's analysis program?"

"Jericho puts the chance of a current or impending cyber attack based on those two incidents happening in the same location at seventeen percent."

"Pretty low."

"It is, based on what we know right now."

Nora didn't have a plan, exactly. The director had also received two separate emails—one from a city official and the other from a concerned citizen. She had the name and addresses for both, but first she wanted to visit the cruise ships. She'd tried to contact both corporate headquarters and individual ship personnel, all with no response.

If they were facing a cyber attack they should have welcomed federal help. Unless the perps had frightened them into silence. It wouldn't be the first time an entity thought paying the ransom and not reporting it to authorities would make the perpetrator go away. That seldom worked. If there was one thing cyber criminals had in common, it was greed.

They wouldn't be satisfied when their initial demands were met.

The first ship they visited, the captain was off site.

The second ship was effectively closed with only a few security guards on board. They claimed to know nothing about why they remained in port.

The third ship they got lucky. The captain was in, and she was willing to talk.

§

Randall admired Nora's dogged determination. When she pursued cyber criminals, she reminded him of a beagle on scent. Nora was good-looking, slim and short, with red hair cut in a shag that framed her face. She had earned her top position in the cyber task force crew, and everyone accepted that she had a special place in the director's heart. Nora's success rate was unparalleled, mainly because she didn't mind risking her life to stop an attack.

Randall felt he was there to watch her back, to pull her back from the edge when she'd gladly sail over it in pursuit of dark forces. He was also the cyber brains of the group. For him, reading code was like listening to a great piece of music. The lines made sense to him, and they always had. Six years enjoying the perks of academia had resulted in a doctoral degree from MIT and a job with the agency.

He preferred working to sitting in a classroom.

Four years with the academy had only whetted his appetite for more action.

His vacation had been nice enough, but one could drink only so many mai tais or stare at so many flawless sunsets. Perhaps his restlessness was owing to the fact that he'd been there with two of his brothers and their families. He loved them all, but they reminded him of what was missing in his life, and Randall wasn't ready to examine that. In truth, he'd missed the action while he was on vacation. It felt good to be chasing the bad guys again, even when he had no idea the nature of the threat they were facing.

Their first break in the case came in the person of Captain Sheila Olson. She looked to be in her late twenties, with short black hair cropped along her neck line, a slim physique, and a no-nonsense attitude.

"Thank you for speaking with us, Captain Olson."

"You can call me Sheila." She leaned back in her chair and studied them.

They were sitting in the captain's office. Located at the top of the ship, it commanded an unparalleled view of Puget Sound.

"Explain to me again who you're with."

Nora and Randall offered their credentials.

After studying then handing them back, the captain drummed her fingers against the desktop. "So you're with the government."

"Cyber Division—security taskforce."

"I'm not even sure that's what we're dealing with. I don't know what it is, and my emails and phone calls to corporate are going unanswered."

Randall and Nora shared a look. A break in the communication lines of an organization's structure was one of the classic hallmarks of a cyber attack.

"Why don't you just tell us what's happened to date, and if we can help, we will."

"What's happened is that all my passengers have cancelled their trips. And it's not just my ship that's experiencing this, as you can see." She nodded toward the windows. "It's getting rather crowded here at the docks, but we can't leave without passengers. There are other boats out there, waiting to dock, waiting to pick up passengers who aren't here."

"And you've spoken with the local government?"

"Why would I do that? It's the passengers who are cancelling. The question is why."

Nora continued asking questions while Randall opened his backpack and pulled out his tablet. His fingers flew over the keyboard. His pulse surged, either from the caffeine he'd ingested or because he was facing a new adversary. That's how he thought of the criminals they pursued—adversaries sitting on the other side of a chessboard. They were locked in battle, each waiting for the other's next move.

"Have you spoken with the other captains?" Nora asked.

"A few. They're as clueless as I am."

"Is this...situation...limited to Seattle?"

"Funny you should ask. I spoke with a captain down in Galveston and another in New Orleans. They're not seeing many cancellations at all—certainly nothing above normal."

"Any idea why corporate isn't responding?"

"I'm assuming they're looking into it, but their complete silence is...unusual."

"I've got something." Randall turned his tablet so they could both see.

"Facebook?" Sheila looked incredulous. "I don't see how..."

"Looks as if someone has started a misinformation campaign. Apparently your ship is... besot with bedbugs."

"What?" Sheila's eyes widened and she leaned

forward, fingertips pressed against the desk. "That's patently untrue."

"A common problem with social media. People often don't know what to believe."

Olson stood, paced toward the windows, then turned back toward Nora and Randall. "So you're telling me that my ship is going down because of *fake news*? I'll issue a press release, and I'll also contact the social media sites, demand they take the posts down."

"It's not as simple as that." Randall returned his tablet to his backpack. "Often these things are started from bogus accounts. They only have to post a few times in strategic groups, and then it's shared by millions of users."

"Millions?" Olson sank back into her chair. "Millions? Then what...what do we do?"

"It's possible that you and the other vessels here in Puget Sound are the victims of a cyber attack. What we need is to interview each captain. Unfortunately, most either haven't been in dock or, if they are, they haven't been willing to speak with us."

"We've been lying low," Olson admitted. "But I'll talk to them. If you can put an end to this, we'll cooperate in any way we can."

Nora handed Olson a business card. "Call me if you think of anything else, and we'd appreciate whatever you can do as far as speaking with the other captains. It's easier to put together the pieces of the puzzle if we have them all."

"Give me an hour."

Randall and Nora headed back toward downtown. As they left the dock area, it seemed to Randall that the bay was even more crowded than it had been when they arrived.

"How are we going to cover all those ships?"

"We're not. I am. You're going back to the hotel to work on tracing down who originally posted the social media content you found."

"And the IP address."

"That too." Nora's voice took on a hard edge. "I have a feeling Miguel Garcia was a few steps ahead of us."

"Or maybe he was involved with the perps. Teachers don't make that much. I'm sure he could've used the cash."

"Either way, there's a connection between his murder two nights ago and what's going on with these cruise ships. Our job is to make that connection, then apprehend and arrest."

"Just like old times." Randall raised his hand to high five Nora. There was a time she would have looked at him blankly and walked away, but that time was long in their past. She shook her head in mock exasperation and slapped her palm against his.

"Just like old times."

~

Chapter Two

Nora woke to the sound of someone banging on her hotel door. Since she slept in shorts and a t-shirt, she didn't bother looking for a robe. After checking through the peep hole to confirm it was Randall, she opened the door and stepped back.

"I found it."

"Found..."

"The connection." He sat on the side of her bed and pushed his tablet into her hands. "It's all there."

She sat next to him, trying not to be irritated that he looked fresh as the proverbial daisy. And was he wearing a designer undershirt? Good grief. She shook her head and turned her gaze to the tablet, trying to understand the connection he'd made. Her brain felt as if it was filled with cobwebs, and she kept blinking to more fully open her eyes. "I thought you were going to sleep."

"I was, but then it occurred to me that the program Miguel Garcia was using to trace the IP address to a location...it doesn't exist."

"How's that possible?"

"Exactly. It means he wrote it, or one of his students did." Randal leaned toward her and pointed to the first window opened on the tablet. "These are newspaper clippings."

"About Garcia and his protégés." Nora scanned the articles he'd found.

"These kids are genius level. Probably Garcia was too. I checked into his background and found that several Fortune 500 companies were clamoring for him to come work for them. The Technical Institute here in Seattle considered it quite a coup when he chose to teach there instead of go into big business."

"Why would he do that?"

"Not for the money, I can guarantee you that. It's a public overflow high school that attracts students who have different aspirations."

"You lost me."

"They don't go out for football or cheerleading or band."

"Ah."

"Instead they're geeks or artists or even a few savants." He took the tablet from her hands and began scrolling until he found the article he wanted, then he shoved it back toward her. "He's had students go to MIT, Cornell, even straight to the upper echelons of Apple without any college degrees."

"Okay." Nora felt suddenly wide awake, but she closed her eyes and willed herself to put the pieces of this op together. She'd only grabbed four hours of sleep, but that was enough. She needed to catch up with Randall, and he was four hours and countless cups of caffeine ahead of her. She opened her eyes and slapped the magnetic cover closed on the tablet. "Talk to me."

"The next window shows..."

"Randall." She stayed his hand on top of the tablet.

He clamped his mouth shut and frowned at her.

"I don't care what's on that screen. Tell me what you found, what you've concluded, and where you think we should go from here."

Randall loved his tech toys, and he still thought his greatest asset was his ability to find and manipulate information. But Nora understood that the reason he'd risen so fast in the agency, the reason he was her partner, was because of the way his brain was able to process that information. Sometimes she had to nudge him away from the tech in order to bring that reasoning to the forefront, because for Randall it was automatic.

He tossed the tablet onto the bed and leaned forward, forearms braced on his knees, eyes staring at the floor. "Garcia was caught up in whatever cyber campaign has been launched against the cruise ships, but not in a way that you'd think. My guess is, one of his current or former students became involved. He was trying to chase them down. Trying to extract them from whatever plot they'd become mired in."

"Okay. That would explain why someone killed him. But why does a cyber terrorist need a couple kids to launch an attack against a fleet of cruise ships, why these ships, why here and why now?"

"Stop thinking of them as kids. They're the best in the industry. Or maybe..." He stood and paced the room. "Maybe the fact that they are kids makes them more susceptible. You don't have a lot of options at that age."

"You have your entire life in front of you at that

age."

"Yes, but it's expected that you follow a certain path. Trust me, I know, and I'm not saying that MIT was a bad choice for me. I'm only saying that some of the kids I knew in high school, some who were as good as me..."

"Doubtful."

He waved that away. "They would have picked a shorter path."

"An easier path."

"In some ways, yeah. Patience isn't a geek's best virtue."

Nora glanced at the clock. The digital display read eight minutes past four. She walked to the phone, picked it up, and ordered two pots of coffee and a variety of items from the breakfast menu.

"Hungry?"

"I have a feeling we need to eat while we can." She sank into the room's only upholstered chair and motioned Randall back where he'd been sitting on the still-made side of the bed. "The captains I spoke with last night—"

"It helped that Sheila Olson managed to get them all in one place."

Nora nodded in agreement. "They'd each been the victim of a social media smear campaign...bed bugs, Norovirus, food poisoning, insolent workers...each attack was different."

"Which kept Facebook's filters from picking up on it. If they'd tried to attack each ship's reputation with the same scheme, they'd have been shut down pretty quickly."

"Why Facebook? I thought the next generation

had moved on to other platforms."

"True, but parents still make up the bulk of consumers, and parents are still on Facebook."

"I'll take your word for that." Nora had never dipped a toe in social media. Her family constantly ragged her about it. They didn't want to have to send an extra text because she wouldn't read their posts on her news feed. "Still no ransom demands."

"Nope."

"But we do know that someone was interrupting each captain's communication to corporate headquarters as well as to the city."

"So their networks were compromised, those emails deleted or diverted." Randall peered at her.

They were at the moment Nora waited for in every operation. The pieces were about to fall into place, if they didn't mess up, if they didn't overlook them, if they acted quickly enough.

Randall pulled at the cuffs of his jeans. He was a strong proponent in looking your best, even when pulling an all-nighter. "When the captains finally resorted to picking up their phones and calling their superiors, evidently those calls were rerouted. That's not easy to do."

"No. It's not." Nora ran her fingers through her hair, which was apparently sticking straight up on one side. "We still have some pretty big questions."

"Who are the students involved?"

"How much did Garcia know?"

"Who killed Garcia?"

"What's the payoff?"

"Are the cruise ships the real target, or only a preliminary target?"

They sat in silence for the next fifteen minutes. At one point Nora glanced up, thinking Randall must have fallen asleep, but he was staring out their fifteenth-floor windows. Staring at the lights of Seattle and the ships in Puget Sound.

A tap on the door interrupted their musings.

"That's breakfast." She opened the door, motioned for Randall to move the food inside, then tipped the server, who didn't look old enough to be working all night.

"I assume the granola and yogurt is for you."

"It is."

"And the bacon and eggs are for me."

"Correct again. Eat up, Randall. It's going to be a long day."

༜

They met with Detective Lawson at seven a.m. in the hotel's dining room. Lawson looked to be in her late-thirties, had brunette hair with blond highlights that was cut as short as Randall's, and a muscular build.

She caught him studying her as they waited for coffee. "You lift?"

"I do. You?" Randall might not be able to jog every day, unless he was chasing cyber criminals, but he had a state-of-the-art weight room at home, and wherever they stayed while on an op, he made good use of the hotel's exercise room.

"Since I was a kid."

"You've kept it up."

"It helps me deal with the stress."

Nora added instant Starbucks coffee to the

steaming coffee mug the waiter brought. "You mean your job isn't relaxed and exciting at the same time? A little banter, a little romance, then you catch the bad guys. I'm sure I saw that on a television show about detectives."

Lawson shrugged her shoulders. "What can I say? I made detective three years ago, and I've rarely had a good night's sleep since."

"Tell us about Garcia."

"Not much to tell. All indications are that it was random street violence."

Randall glanced at Nora who nodded once.

"We think he was tracking down a student."

"Why?"

"We're still piecing that together."

Nora sat back and crossed her arms. "It has to do with his phone logs, internet activity, and the crowded state of Puget Sound."

"Everyone's wondering about that. What's going on out there?"

"Disinformation campaign being raged on social medial."

"Huh."

"Do you get much of that here?" Randall already knew the history of cyber attacks in Seattle. It had been one of the first things he'd researched the night before. Often a cyber perp would be paid off then come back for more.

"Cyber terrorism isn't really my department. According to the Office of Emergency Management we experience daily threats, but we have yet to experience a large-scale attack."

"They wouldn't necessarily tell you about such

a thing if it had happened." Nora splayed her hands out flat on the table, stared at them a minute, and then looked up. "Have you noticed anything unusual? Cell phones not working, computers going down, rolling brownouts, a dramatic slow-down in network performance?"

"Nothing like that. So you're suggesting this is more than a random act of violence?"

"Definitely more. Was his wallet taken?"

"Yes, as well as his watch and wedding ring."

"So, someone wanted it to look like a burglary gone bad."

"The bullet to the head was a little excessive, at least that's what we thought at first. But someone on PCP or Oxy? There's really no understanding why they do what they do."

"Medical Examiner's report?"

"We'll have it this afternoon."

They spoke another ten minutes about Garcia's background, which was clean, and Seattle crime stats, which weren't any higher than any other tourist town. Finally Nora motioned for the waiter to bring the bill. "We'd appreciate it if you'd share the results from the ME with us as soon as you have them."

"Of course."

"Keep your eyes open for any type of tech anomaly, and if there's anyone you trust implicitly ask them to do the same."

"How big do you think this is?"

"Based on the evidence we have at this point, I couldn't say with any measure of certainty."

"But our best guess is that it's big." Randall looked again out the plate glass windows, looked at a city that was waking and going to work like any other day. In the time since he'd been partnered with Nora, he'd learned that it was usually the most normal-looking day that exploded into utter chaos.

Better to brace yourself and meet it head on.

୨

Chapter Three

Randall felt like Gulliver standing in the midst of a crowd of Lilliputians. Students flowed around them on both sides, crowding the walk—loud, boisterous, young. The Technical Institute might be home to geeks, near-geniuses, and savants, but it was still a high school. Students of every size, shape, and color swarmed toward the front door of the building.

He practically jogged to keep up with Nora. He'd yet to figure out how she could move so quickly given how much shorter and smaller she was. His stride was twice hers, though that didn't help as they dodged students on skateboards, others wearing tennis shoes with rollers, and clueless couples with their arms wrapped around one another. "Does it make you wish you were young again?"

"Not a chance."

"I pegged you for the type who loved high school."

"Couldn't escape fast enough."

"I kind of liked it."

"Of course you did. Let me guess, star football player."

"Well, yeah, but..."

"Lots of girls vying to go to the school dance with you."

"I guess."

"Teacher's pet?"

"I was a good student. What did you do, interview my school counselor?"

"Lucky guess."

Ten minutes later they were sitting in the principal's office. Randall was a grown man, plus he was an MIT grad and held a coveted spot on the agency's cyber division squad. So why was he experiencing the classic signs of guilt...dry mouth, twitching muscle in his left jaw, and he couldn't stop jiggling his right leg? Being in a principal's office—any principal's office— made him nervous.

Nora, on the other hand, looked as if she'd spent plenty of time sitting across from the principal, and the thought obviously didn't bother her a bit. He really did need to find out more about her past.

"Thank you for meeting with us, Principal Nguyen."

It was impossible to guess Nguyen's age. She had flawless skin, raven black hair pulled back with a simple elastic band, and she dressed nearly as well as Randall did. Perhaps educational jobs paid better than he'd thought.

"We're bereft at the loss of Mr. Garcia. He was a well-liked professor and highly respected colleague. To think that he died from some random act of violence, well, it's hard to conceive."

"We're not sure it was so random." Nora waited as Nguyen processed that piece of information.

Randall noticed a slight tightening in the skin around her eyes and a stiffening of her spine.

"Go on."

"My partner and I believe Mr. Garcia may have been trying to help a current or former student."

"We have good students here. I can't imagine how this could involve any of them."

Nora glanced at Randall, silently handing the ball off to him.

"Some of your students attend this particular high school because they have trouble fitting in elsewhere, correct?"

Nguyen pierced him with a glare. "Our students come here because they are an asset to the program and the program helps them to develop their special skills."

"Of course, but perhaps because of those special skills, they don't always fit into a traditional environment. Wouldn't you say that's true?"

"Possibly."

Randall didn't like to share his own history. He didn't like tooting his own horn. His parents had gone to great lengths to treat him like any other kid. But perhaps now wasn't the time for modesty. "I scored 165 on the IQ test, and no, it wasn't administered at my school. My parents had me tested because I was inattentive in class. My SAT scores were 1580. When I ask if your students have trouble fitting in, I speak from experience."

Nora gave him a reproachful look. "You told me you were on the football team."

"Another activity my parents thought would help me fit in, and it did—to a point. But academically I needed more, and that wasn't easy to find where I grew up."

Nguyen seemed to relax, if only minutely. "I'm sorry if I took your question defensively. Many people don't understand the challenges our students face. We provide an important conduit for them to travel from teenager to adult. Do we have some students who struggle more than others? Of course. All schools do."

"Anyone that particularly stands out in your mind?" Nora asked. "Someone who might have been a protégé of Mr. Garcia's?"

"I can't think of anyone, but you really should speak with our counselor. My job is increasingly administrative, and I don't mind saying that I resent that. I chose this vocation because I wanted to help students. Now I rarely see them or interact with them at all."

"Could we possibly meet with the counselor today?"

"You can meet with him now."

Randall expected the counselor to be a harried man with files stacked on his desk and students waiting outside his door. Instead they were ushered into an office that broke all of those stereotypes. The desk was meticulously clean, with the pencils aligned straight on the top and a fresh pad of paper next to them. A tablet sat docked on a station. LeBron Davis stood and shook their hands. African American, easily in his fifties if the white in his hair was any indication, and probably less than a hundred and forty pounds.

Davis didn't invite them to sit. From the expression on his face, it would seem he couldn't get rid of them fast enough. "How can I help you?"

Nora explained what they were looking for and

why. Before she'd made it halfway through her spiel, Davis was shaking his head.

"We take the privacy of our students very seriously. I can't give you any of that information without a court order."

Randall braced himself for Nora's response. She didn't like being stymied on an investigation.

To his surprise, she simply sat in the chair across from Davis and folded her hands on top of one another in her lap. Randall sat as well. Davis closed his eyes as if he needed to muster a massive amount of patience. How did this guy make it as a school counselor?

"I'm sorry that you wasted your time coming here. Miss Wilson will escort you back to the front lobby." He reached to touch a button on his phone, no doubt one that would summon the elderly Miss Wilson who had shown them in.

Nora held up a finger.

Davis's hand hovered over the phone's button.

"We're not leaving."

"Excuse me?"

"I said, we're not leaving." Nora now pointed her finger at him. "We're trying to stop a major cyber attack in your city, and while I respect the privacy of your students, what I'm asking for is not an invasion of that privacy. I want the names and addresses of students who are or were of particular interest to Miguel Garcia. If they left this school prematurely, I want notations explaining that departure. Ms. Nguyen assured us that you could supply us with that information."

Davis shifted uncomfortably in his chair. "I'm not sure I can give you what you want."

"You can and you will, because we're investigating

the murder of one of your colleagues. Were you to impede that investigation, I would have to pull you in for questioning." Nora glanced around the office.

Randall followed her gaze and became aware of what he hadn't noticed until that point. The office wasn't just clean, it was compulsively in order.

Not a speck of dust.

Every book meticulously lined up on the shelves.

And while Davis wasn't dressed as well as his boss, his clothes had been fastidiously pressed. Randall could just imagine four more identical sets of clothes lined up in his closet, hangers spaced a quarter inch apart.

How did the man ever stand the chaos of students?

Perhaps he didn't.

Perhaps he stayed in his office and shuffled papers, carefully and methodically. No, that didn't fit. Principal Nguyen had struck him as someone who didn't abide fools. The man must be proficient at his job or he wouldn't have it. Still, he definitely exhibited obsessive compulsive tendencies, something Nora had picked up on right away. Apparently she planned to take full advantage of the man's condition.

"Should we have to take you in for questioning, I believe you'd find the Seattle interrogation rooms less to your liking than..." She spread her hands out to encompass his office. "Than this."

Thirty minutes later, they left the building with the file.

᠀

As they walked back to their rental car, it seemed to Nora that the sun shone brighter, the trees were an almost unbearable green, and the scent of the Pacific was practically overpowering. Everything was so...alive. Once again they were at the crossroads of an investigation. Turn the wrong way and tomorrow's headlines would be filled with tragedy and disaster. Turn the right way, and they'd win against the forces of anarchy.

Nora felt they were getting closer to the center of the impending disaster, but they weren't getting there fast enough.

"Deep thoughts?"

"Very." She glanced at her partner. He was a hulking guy that she trusted implicitly, and she was glad Randall Goodwin was the agent at her side today. "That list is too long."

"Twenty-four students. I wouldn't have thought that many would have bailed. This is a swanky facility."

"But like you said, they'd have trouble adjusting, and look at that list. Eighty percent report that they traded in their school I.D. for homeschooling."

"They won't develop social skills that way."

"No, but for some students, it might be the only way they stay in school at all."

"So how are we going to narrow it down?"

"We need to get inside Garcia's head."

"Only one way to do that."

"Yup. Let's go visit his widow."

She knew Randall didn't like interviewing the family of the deceased. He'd told her as much the other two times they'd had to do so. Both times left him nervous and awkward, as if dealing with people in their grief somehow propelled him back to a previous time—a time when he was still self-conscious and socially inept. He'd shared with her only a little of what his teenage years had been like, and it was hard for her to imagine. He was so confident now—so assured. Ninety-five percent of the time, he gave off the demeanor of a relaxed jock.

He fumbled with his seatbelt as she put Garcia's address into her phone's GPS program. "It's just that the days immediately following a death are intensely personal."

"I'm aware." Nora started the car, checked both directions, then pulled out into traffic.

"I hate to intrude."

"As do I, but we can't allow social conventions to keep us from solving this case."

He didn't have an argument for that. They drove in silence for the next twenty minutes. The neighborhood they pulled into was modestly upscale. Garcia's home was a bungalow style that looked as if it had been built in the sixties and recently remodeled.

A line of cars stretched out of the driveway and down the street.

"Uh-oh. Looks like she has company." Randall cringed as Nora parallel parked the suburban in a space barely large enough to contain it.

"Then we'll make this quick."

Carmen Garcia was five and a half feet tall and fifty pounds overweight. She reminded Nora of everyone's grandma, but her face was pale and drawn, her eyes rimmed with red.

After introducing herself and Randall, Nora said, "I'm sorry to intrude today of all days..."

"The funeral is tomorrow. *Mi familia*, and Miguel's, they are coming from all over the country."

"I understand, but it's important that we talk to you, and I'm afraid it can't wait."

Carmen squinted up into the sun, then stepped out on the front porch and motioned toward wicker furniture with brightly colored cushions. "It's crowded inside. Perhaps we could speak here."

"First, we'd like to offer our condolences."

"Miguel, he was a friend to everyone. I can't understand who would do this. Why anyone would do this." Carmen reached into the pocket of her slacks and pulled out a package of Kleenex. Plucking one from the package, she swiped at her eyes. "Is that why you're here? Are you going to find who killed Miguel?"

"We're going to try, but we're here to talk to you about his students."

Carmen's head popped up. "I don't understand."

"We think Miguel may have been trying to help a student, that maybe that's why he was in the dock area the night of his murder."

"But the police said it was a robbery."

"And that is a possibility." Nora glanced at Randall. She needed his help here. Carmen was clearly on the fence as far as sharing anything important with them. Two could be more persuasive than one.

Randall intertwined his fingers together, in a prayer-like posture. "Mrs. Garcia—"

"You may call me Carmen." Her voice had softened, though she continued dabbing at her eyes.

"Carmen, we're so sorry to have to ask you these questions today of all days. This is a day that you should be celebrating Miguel's life even as you mourn his passing."

"We were going to purchase an RV and travel through the northwest." Instead of producing more tears, the pronouncement seemed to firm her resolve. She sat up straighter, clasped her hands in her lap, and met Randall's gaze, then Nora's. "If I can help you find why this happened, who did this...then I will. My grief will be with me a long time, but now is the time to catch whoever is responsible."

Nora nodded. "That's what we want as well. As I said, we think this may have something to do with one of Miguel's students. Is there someone that he seemed worried about? Someone he spoke of recently?"

"Miguel watched over his students like a mother hen. Even after they left the Institute—and some do, you know." She stared out over the front yard, past the neighborhood, to the water of Puget Sound shimmering in the distance. "Even when they left, he would stay in contact with them, encouraging them and trying to find other places for them to learn or work. Having extraordinary intelligence as so many of his students did, it's not always an easy thing."

"We have a list." Nora motioned for Randall to hand her the piece of paper. "Do any of these names sound familiar?"

"They all do. Miguel believed in interacting with his students, being a real mentor to them. He tried to invite each student to our house for dinner...we would do it in small groups so that all of them could attend within a year."

Randall met Nora's gaze. They were getting a more complete picture of the man who was the key to whatever was happening. He was intensely committed to his students. He seemed to view his responsibility to them as a calling.

"All of these names are students he spoke of." Carmen ran a finger down the sheet, then glanced up at Nora and Randall. "But these aren't his current students. These are students who had problems...students who left."

"That's correct."

"This one." She tapped the sheet. "Miguel mentioned him to me just a few nights ago."

Randall craned his neck to better see what name she was pointing at. "Jonathan Coleman?"

"Jonathan was a favorite of Miguel's. He said that Jonathan..." She pulled in a shaky breath and willed herself to go on. "Miguel said that Jonathan reminded him of a younger version of himself. My husband was sure that Jonathan could go far."

A tingle crept down Nora's spine. "Was your husband upset when Jonathan left the Institute?"

"He was always saddened when students made choices he didn't agree with. Three nights ago..." Carmen glanced up and again stared out past the row of cars lining the street, squinting her eyes in an effort to remember. "He told me he'd learned something that concerned him, and that he needed to contact Jonathan, needed to be sure that the boy was all right."

"And did he? Contact him?"

"He tried. He emailed and phoned, but Jonathan didn't answer either. I thought that was the end of it."

"Thank you, Carmen. You've been very helpful." Nora pulled out a business card and handed it to Miguel's wife as she and Randall stood. "If you think of anything else, anything at all, please call me at that number."

Carmen nodded. Randall and Nora started down the walk, but turned back at the sound of her voice. "Find who did this. Find the person who has brought this tragedy upon our home, our family. Promise me that you will do that."

"We'll try." Which suddenly seemed inadequate to Nora. There were so many good people in the world. When their lives were touched by tragedy, by persons without scruples, she felt it was her personal responsibility to bring those guilty parties to justice—man or woman, someone working alone or in tandem with others.

Her job was to find them and get them off the street.

What happened to them after that wasn't her concern.

Nora didn't give much thought to how the legal system handled the perps she turned over to them. She trusted, perhaps naively, that the process of justice would move as it should. But that process began here, on the street, with her and Randall.

"I have the distinct feeling we're running out of time."

"Same."

Nora plugged Jonathan's address into her phone, surprised to see it was located on the other side of town and not surprised to see it was fairly near the docks. Another piece of the puzzle slipped into piece. It might not explain who had killed Garcia, but it explained why he was there.

"Are you watching your normal channels, looking for bumps or unusual activity on cyber fronts?"

"I am. I also wrote a program last night that's more specific to Seattle."

"When did you sleep?"

He waved that idea away. "I'll catch up when this is over."

She grunted at that idea as they pulled out on the road. "If this is a cyber attack, and to me it's looking increasingly like it is, then it can't be about cruise ships."

"Agreed."

"Especially empty cruise ships. They'd make a much juicier target if they were full of passengers."

"So what's the point?"

"It's a distraction. It has to be."

"And as we're running down that problem…"

"They attack on another front." She glanced over at him. "Where else is Seattle uniquely vulnerable?"

"They're a tech center." Randall tapped and scrolled past various screens on his phone. "They've added more tech jobs in the last two years than any other city."

"All right. That could make them a big juicy target in some weirdo's mind."

"Silicon Valley seems to be fleeing to Seattle."

"Explain that to me."

"Amazon and Microsoft have a presence here, as do Alphabet and Facebook, plus a wide range of tech startups."

"Why Seattle?"

"Affordable housing."

"Seriously?"

"Compared to California, plus Washington has no state income tax." Randall frowned at his phone. "Not everyone is happy about that growth. Median

Vannetta Chapman

rentals have seen a big jump, cost of living is up overall, and the traffic..."

They both stared at the snarl of traffic they'd landed in. "I can't believe we're having this problem at ten thirty in the morning. Why aren't these people at work?"

"Maybe our perp is a Seattle native who doesn't approve of the changes."

"Or a survivalist who thinks tech is going to bring about the collapse of civilization."

"We just had one of those. Isn't it time for something different?"

The bantering helped ease the tension in her shoulders. Still, there was something they were missing, and that made her antsy. She could prepare for what she could envision, but the thing they hadn't thought of? That was harder to tackle.

"Huh." Randall tapped a few more times on his phone, then looked up at her.

"Find something?"

"Ninety percent of Seattle's electricity is produced using hydropower."

"That's a good thing, right?"

"It is unless you're an Orca whale." Randall spent the rest of the drive looking at the environmental protests regarding the Lower Snake River dams.

He read her stories about Tahlequah, the mother orca who carried her dead calf a thousand miles, and how the entirety of Washington state became embroiled in preserving one of the Northwest's most iconic symbols.

As he read, Nora considered whether they could be dealing with an environmentalist who'd decided to take things into their own hands. Possibly.

Certainly there had been environmental controversies surrounding cruise ships. She wasn't ready to jump that direction yet, but hopefully Jonathan Coleman could shed some light on what threat they were facing.

The fact that they were depending on a high school dropout for guidance didn't surprise her one bit.

Chapter Four

Randall rechecked the address on the sheet against the address on the door. "It's not unusual for poor students with extraordinary abilities to attend a school like the Institute."

"What makes you say that?"

"If they were wealthy, their parents would already have transferred them to a private school or have them attend a local school and work with tutors."

"Is that what your parents did?"

"Transfer me? No. Pop wanted me to be in a normal school. It was mom who insisted that we hire the tutors, and that probably kept me in school more than anything else. They were able to...challenge me."

The government housing project they were looking at wasn't the worst Randall had ever seen, but it was close.

When they knocked on the door to 27B, there was a pause as someone called out, "Who is it?"

"We're government agents. We need to ask Jonathan Coleman a few questions."

Randall glanced at Nora and knew they were

both thinking the same thing. If Jonathan Coleman was at this address, he might decide to run. They'd checked for a back entrance, and there didn't appear to be one. Just as Randall was thinking he should walk around the building again, they heard the sound of locks being disengaged and the door opened.

Randall didn't believe in stereotypes. He'd been the victim of one too often. Still, he was surprised that the young man in front of them was clean-cut and appeared to be somewhat athletic.

No glasses.

No acne.

He wasn't dressed in a dirty t-shirt with a nerd slogan.

"I'm Jonathan Coleman." His voice was hesitant, and his body blocked any view of the room beyond.

"Can we come in?" Nora asked.

Jonathan glanced back into the small apartment. "What's this about?"

"We're investigating a possible terror attack here in the city, and we think you may be able to help us."

Jonathan's expression relaxed at the words *terror attack*. Not the response they got from most people. "I wouldn't know anything about that."

"Then we won't stay long."

Jonathan nodded once and stepped back. "My grandma is sleeping, so we'll need to keep it down."

"Of course."

As they walked into the room, Randall noticed several things at once—the neatly folded sheet and blankets next to the couch, the smell of bacon and eggs, and the jump rope and hand weights stored on a shelf under the television. Jonathan had apparently been sitting on the couch, working on a laptop. He closed the device and placed it carefully on the coffee table.

The upholstery was threadbare, but the room was painfully clean. Someone was making a heroic attempt to create a home in the cramped space.

"Why do you think I can help you?"

"Is it okay if we sit?" Randall didn't want to spook the kid. He'd learned from Nora that people were less defensive, and less prone to make a run for it, if they were sitting.

"I guess."

"You were Miguel Garcia's student, correct? When you attended the Institute?" Nora looked down at the list of students Lebron Davis had given them, as if she needed to check it to be sure.

"Yeah. Why do you ask?"

Nora folded the sheet and handed it back to Randall. "Did you know that Mr. Garcia was killed three nights ago?"

"What?"

There was no faking the look of shock on Jonathan's face. He definitely hadn't known about Garcia's murder, though he could have been involved without realizing it. Randall had seen crazier things.

"Are you sure?" Jonathan wiped his palms against his jeans. "I mean, are you sure? Oh man. That can't be right. Maybe it was a different Miguel Garcia."

"We just visited with his wife, Carmen." Randall tucked the list of students into his pocket.

"How...how is she? Man. I can't believe that he's really dead. Everyone loved Miguel. Who would do such a thing? How is Carmen?"

"Carmen's upset, as you'd expect. She had a lot of

family with her."

Nora scooted forward on the chair, propped her elbows on her legs and clasped her hands together. "Jonathan, Carmen told us that Miguel was trying to get in touch with you on the night he was murdered."

Jonathan froze in his seat. When he tried to speak, he cleared his throat twice, then said, "What? No. I hadn't heard from him."

"He emailed and called. He even left a message on your cell phone."

"I don't have that cell phone anymore. They went up on their rates, and...well, most people just send a text nowadays. I can receive those on my computer."

"You have a pretty nice laptop." Randall could tell that it was the newest Mac model, and they weren't cheap.

Jonathan licked his lip, glanced at the laptop, then at Nora, and finally settled his gaze on Randall. "I was doing some work for a guy. He paid me with the laptop. If it's hot, I didn't know it, but...uh...I didn't exactly ask for a receipt."

"What kind of work did you do for him?"

"Some simple coding for an accounting program. That was six months ago though."

"About the time you dropped out of school?" Nora asked.

"Yeah." When Nora didn't follow up with another question, just waited expectantly for him to explain, he added, "My grandma, she had a stroke and needed someone to be at home with her."

"Where are your parents?"

"No idea. Mom stops by a couple times a year. I haven't seen my dad since I was a kid."

Randall had to bite back the words *you still are a kid*. Instead he said, "That must be tough."

"Whatever. Look, I don't think I can help you with a terror attack. I dropped out of TI because I needed to be here. I wasn't going to let them put my grandma in some kind of state run nursing home. Maybe you're really with social services, but if you are I've been doing all my lessons."

A laugh escaped Randall's lips.

"If you don't believe me, I'll show you."

"We're not with social services, and it's not that I don't believe you. It's that I know from experience how long it probably takes you to do your school work." He put the last two words in air quotes. "Do you actually do it, or did you write a program to make it appear that you're online?"

Jonathan's eyes widened, and Nora looked at Randall accusingly. "You told me you attended high school."

"I did, but a couple classes I took online so I'd have time for my own hobbies."

"You look like you played football," Jonathan said.

"Guilty as charged, but I was also into coding, like you. I wrote a program to make the online portal think I was logged in and active, then spent the time working on something that actually challenged me."

Jonathan didn't seem to know what to say about that, so instead he stood and stuck his hands in his pockets.

"I really don't think I can help with whatever you're after."

"Sit down, Jonathan." Nora's voice brokered no

argument.

Randall would have sat down if he'd been standing, but to give Jonathan credit the kid wasn't backing down.

"I can't help you."

"You need to tell us what you know. We're trying to catch whoever killed Miguel, and we're trying to stop a cyber attack."

"What kind of cyber attack?" Jonathan's gaze darted toward the front door, then the window, then back at Nora.

"Jonathan, look at me." Randall kept his voice low and calm. "Don't try to run. I will catch you, and then we just have to haul you in. So don't try to run."

"Why would I run?"

"You tell us." Nora sat back and crossed her arms. "Tell us what you know about the murder of Miguel Garcia."

"I don't know anything. I didn't even know he was dead." Jonathan collapsed more than sat on the couch. His face was a picture of misery.

"He died just a few blocks from here." Nora's voice had softened. "Are you sure you haven't talked to him in the last week?"

"No. And I haven't checked my email in months because it's all spam. No one uses email anyway. But if he was killed here...do you think he was coming to see me?"

"Carmen said he was worried about you. Why would that be?"

Jonathan's eyes darted toward the laptop then back at the aged carpet. "No idea."

"Jonathan..." Nora waited for him to glance up at

her, and Randall knew what was coming. She was losing her patience and she was about to unload on him. Kid or not, they were running out of time.

"Randall understands your background, but I don't, and I don't need to. I don't really care if you're bored at school or working under the table for someone. That's not because I'm an uncaring person, and it's not because you don't matter. I don't care, at this point in time, because I have to stop the people who are about to unleash a cyber attack on the Seattle area. Those attacks don't just affect devices. They affect people, and I swore to protect those people against that very thing."

"I don't...it's just that...look..." He glanced up, eyes wide, face paled, right arm shaking slightly. "All I did was post some stuff to social media. It didn't hurt anyone, and these people...they paid really well. It's not even that hard to do, and I mean...I don't even think it's illegal."

"You posted about the cruise ships?"

"Yeah."

"So you could be sued for libel by some very large corporations."

"No. I just...I mean maybe it was just my opinion. Don't we have a First Amendment in this country?"

"Doesn't cover defamation that is objectively false, published, and causes financial injury." Nora ticked off the three requirements on her fingers.

"Who hired you?" Randall asked.

"I have no idea. I saw the job on the Z boards."

"Z boards?" Nora shook her head. "You lost me."

"Geeks pick up work there," Randall explained. "How are they paying you?"

"Half the money was dropped in my PayPal

account when I agreed to the job. I get the other half tomorrow."

"Why tomorrow?"

"Because the job's over tomorrow. I only have to keep the social media activity going until daybreak."

"What happens then?" Nora's back had gone ramrod straight.

"I don't know." Jonathan spoke more emphatically. "And how could some false news stories about cruise ships hurt anyone? How could that even be classified as a cyber attack?"

"Because the cruise ship stories are just a diversion, though a very big one at this moment." Randall picked up the laptop and handed it to him. "Log in to your PayPal account and let me see the payment receipt."

As Randall studied the details of the payment, Jonathan's grandmother peeked around the corner of the room. She was old, frail, and more than a little confused.

"Jonathan? Is that your momma and dad? Have they come to visit?"

"No, grandma. It's just some people from my school." Jonathan hopped up and ushered his grandmother back into her room, talking softly and assuring her that everything was all right.

Randall met Nora's gaze.

He hadn't missed the reference to daybreak. If what the kid said was true and it was related to this thing they were chasing, they had less than eighteen hours to stop the attack.

৩

Chapter Five

Nora paced back and forth as Randall pulled a small device from his pocket and plugged it into Jonathan's laptop. She saw the scene flash to black, then fill with lines of code. Randall was in his element. He smiled to himself, and his fingers flew over the keyboard as he explained to Jonathan that he was tracing the source of the payment.

"How is that possible?"

"Watch and learn, grasshopper."

Moments later Randall relayed the information to the director's office, then told Jonathan what he wanted him to do.

Nora was growing impatient. Chasing code was all good and fine, but there was someone out there in the real world intent on creating chaos. They needed to get on the road. "Can't we just take the laptop with us?"

"Apparently I've been compromised. They're tracking my computer, which means they'd know if you took it with you." Jonathan stared at the screen in disbelief. "How did I not see this?"

"Kind of hard to see what's hidden. Unless you

can look at the code there's no way you would know, and obviously the laptop developers would rather you stay out of that side of the device."

"Hence your plug-in, literally."

"You got it." Randall high-fived the young man.

Nora didn't know whether to roll her eyes or throttle them both. She settled for a stern look and a gruff reminder. "We're on a time clock here. Something else is happening. We don't know where. We don't know who, and we don't know..."

"Classmates."

Nora and Jonathan both stared at Randall in confusion.

"Our perp used a student from the Institute the first time. Maybe he dipped into that well twice." Randall pulled the sheet of paper out of his pocket and passed it to Jonathan. "Tell me who on that paper is smarter than you are, and don't be shy. I know you know."

He glanced up at Nora and said, "Most geeks are aware of where they stand in the pecking order."

Jonathan barely glanced at the list. "Only person on there who can code better than I can was Kathryn Waters."

"Was?"

Jonathan shrugged. "We don't talk. I have no idea what she's doing now. Kathryn is...somewhat antisocial."

Randall gave him a few final words of instruction. As he and Nora headed to the door, Jonathan asked, "How did he know? How did Professor Garcia know that I was...involved in something?"

"Best guess? He wrote a program to keep track of his students. He cared about you, Jonathan."

"Yeah, and it cost him his life."

Nora glanced at Randall, walked back across the room, and squatted down in front of Jonathan. He reminded Nora of her nephew, and she realized with a start that she wanted to see him again, that it had been much too long and she'd taken certain things—like family—for granted.

Not that long ago, she'd been in a small town in Shipshewana, Indiana, chasing yet another cyber criminal. In that case, she'd had to depend on the help of an Amish farmer. Benjamin Lapp had reminded her that family and faith matter. She'd promised herself she'd make those things a priority in her life, and she'd meant to. But they'd been pushed aside. She could only hope and pray that she'd have another chance, that this op wouldn't be her last.

Now she looked at Jonathan and said the words that she hoped were what he needed to hear.

"We're not responsible for what criminals do. We don't cause it. We don't do anything to deserve it, but if we're lucky...and if we're very good at what we do... we can stop it."

She waited until Jonathan looked up and nodded. The tears in his eyes tore at her heart, but she'd given him as much time as she could. He had family in the other room—even if it was only a grandmother he was caring for.

He was a smart kid.

He'd figure life out.

As they jogged to the car, Nora tossed the keys to Randall. "You drive."

"You got it, boss."

Which did cause her to roll her eyes. She was

not Randall's boss. She'd told him that multiple times, which seemed to provoke him to use the term even more.

As they headed toward the address listed for Kathryn, the neighborhoods went from poor to gentrified to wealthy. Nora tried to work out the possible scenarios they could be dealing with as she waited for her call to be pushed through to the director.

When he picked up, she tapped the speaker button. "I have you on speaker. Randall and I are following up another lead."

"Our only other lead," Randall muttered.

"Looks like you've landed in the middle of something big."

"Do we have confirmation?"

"Still no chatter, but we checked into the cruise ships and there's no doubt their comms were intercepted. We're holding off alerting the social media sites to what's happening...don't want to spook whoever is behind this."

"Sites?"

"What Randall found was the tip of the iceberg. They've infiltrated all the main ones using a variety of unusual techniques. We'll shut it down as soon as you've caught the perp."

"I appreciate your confidence, but we don't even know who we're chasing."

"You rarely do."

She updated him on what they'd learned from Jonathan, their suspicions that this could be the work of an environmental activist, and told him where they were headed next.

"Back up teams are in route, but if what you

suspect is true, they won't get there in time to be much help."

The director signed off as they pulled up in front of a mansion.

"Why would someone this wealthy attend a public school?"

"Sometimes parents think it'll help them adjust... it rarely works."

"Because..."

"Do you think someone who lives here will fit in with someone like Jonathan?"

"People from different backgrounds can..."

"Yes, they can, but they rarely do."

Their knock on the door was answered by a maid, complete with uniform and a duster in her hand. Five minutes later, they were settled in the formal sitting room with Mrs. Waters asking if they'd like tea. Nora felt like she'd fallen into a poorly written British novel.

"Actually we're here to speak with Kathryn. Is she home?"

"She is, but Kathryn is...fragile. I'm afraid I need a little more information if you expect to see her."

Nora mentally calculated the time it would take to give a full explanation versus pulling her weapon and threatening the woman. Fortunately, Randall rescued her from her own impatience, quickly explained the situation, and emphasized that it was urgent they speak with Kathryn immediately.

After examining their credentials closely, Mrs. Waters stood and straightened her close fitting skirt. Nora was surprised the woman could even walk in the outfit she had on. Why would anyone dress that way at home? Stiletto heels only added to the ludicrous picture.

"I suspect you're wasting your time. Kathryn hasn't had access to the internet since the last incident." She led them through the kitchen, out the back door, to a cottage that was larger than Nora's apartment. "The counselor said it would help Kathryn if she had her own space, so we moved her out here. I trust if you need anything, you'll let me know."

A carefully tended garden surrounded the swimming pool in front of them.

Randall grinned at her. "We meet all kinds in this job."

"Indeed we do."

Kathryn answered the door after they'd rung the buzzer multiple times. Nora was once again tempted to pull her weapon and shoot out the lock. She probably needed a vacation. Her irritation levels were off the chart, and it didn't help when she got her first look at Kathryn.

The girl had raven black hair with putrid green streaks that fell in front of her eyes. More rings and studs adorned her face than Nora cared to count.

She pushed her way inside. "We need to talk."

"About what? I don't even know who you are."

Randall had walked straight to the laptop. When he picked it up, Kathryn pounced. Nora had the girl pinned against the wall before she'd made it within three feet of Randall.

"Your mother tells us you have no internet access because of a prior incident. Care to explain what you're doing on the laptop?"

Kathryn opened and shut her mouth twice before settling on, "Whatever" and collapsing onto the couch.

Nora was giving her the short version of who they were and what they were looking for when Randall interrupted her.

"You need to see this."

Kathryn made an attempt to join them, but Nora barked "Stay" and surprisingly, the girl did.

Randall had lined up multiple open windows, all with specifications of dams along the lower Snake River and all noted as orca foraging range.

"Get this information to the director." She turned on Kathryn with the force and fury of a Midwestern storm. "I want to know what you're planning, when it's happening, and who is behind this."

Kathryn had stood up. Now she smirked in Nora's direction, pushed a recording button on her phone, and held up her hands in surrender. "We're now on a live twitter feed, in case you're wondering, and I'm formally requesting a lawyer."

Nora snatched the phone from her hand, turned off the recording and tossed the device to Randall who caught it with his left while he continued to type with his right. Her partner's athletic abilities came in handy at times. She recognized the thought for what it was— her brain's way of dealing with a situation that was quickly spiraling out of control.

"Stop. This not a television show or a live stream." She crossed the room to where Kathryn was standing and kept going, forcing the girl to walk backwards until her back was against the wall. "This is real life, Kathryn, and we operate under the power of the U.S. government and with the full force of the anti-terrorism legislative acts. You do not want to mess with me, because I promise you, I will win."

"That's what you people always think." Something savage crossed Kathryn's face. Nora had the thought that she should back up, that perhaps she'd cornered something she wasn't prepared to deal with; then she remembered the dams on the laptop, and she pushed harder.

"What people is that? The ones protecting your country?"

"This country isn't mine. I didn't create the borders and I don't support the current totalitarian regime."

"Totalitarian regime..." Nora closed her eyes and tried to summon up enough patience to not throttle the girl.

Kathryn took advantage of Nora's temporary lapse in attention and dodged left, then around Nora and out the front door.

Randall glanced up. "Want me to..."

"I've got this." Nora sprinted out of the cottage, her pulse pounding and muscles relieved to finally have a way to express the pent up adrenaline. She caught the girl between a cabana and a hot tub. Within two minutes, she had Kathryn's hands zip-tied behind her, had marched her back into the cottage, and motioned for her to sit back on the couch.

"Tell me what you know, or I will personally see that you are tried as an adult."

"Tried for what? I haven't done anything."

"Thirty years to life, Kathryn. And they won't let you dye your hair or wear your piercings or bring in your personal hotspot for internet connectivity. It'll all go away, for a very long time."

"People like you are what's wrong with this country."

"Tell me...everything."

She didn't tell them everything—that was obvious. But she told them enough. Mostly she thought she lectured them, clarifying to the older generation all that they'd done wrong and the myriad ways they were destroying the Earth. But she let a name slip and also a few details, no doubt in an effort to show her superiority.

Nora had a clear picture now, and she understood what they were up against. The first thing they needed was help. The director's teams were in the air, and Nora didn't want to take the time to brief the local federal officers. So instead she pulled out her phone and called Julia Lawson.

"Still looking into Garcia's murder?"

"I haven't solved it, if that's what you mean." Nora gave her the address to Kathryn's home.

"Do you think she was involved in his murder?"

"I'm not sure the degree of her involvement, but she knows something about it. My guess is that she had a way to track Garcia, that she was aware he was keeping tabs on his ex-students, and that she alerted whoever she was working for. I think a conspiracy to murder charge might hold up."

Kathryn visibly paled.

"We got the ballistics back." Lawson shuffled papers on her desk. "You were right—it wasn't a robbery. Both the caliber of the shot and the distance it was made from indicate his murder was something other than a random act of violence."

"So a professional."

"Looks like it."

"Randall's working on Kathryn's computer now. I need you to babysit her for me and ensure that she does not have access to the internet for the next twenty-four hours." She looked directly at Kathryn as she spoke. The girl was obviously rattled, although Nora doubted that would cause her to reveal any more than she had. "After twenty-four hours, she's all yours."

As she disconnected the call, she glanced around and noticed for the first time the images of Orcas that permeated Kathryn's cottage. They were inlaid in the Italian tile, woven into the coasters on the table, even tattooed on Kathryn's arm. She walked over to the girl, forced herself to remember that she was just that—a girl who had no idea what damage she could cause.

But perhaps that was wrong.

Perhaps Kathryn knew exactly what she was doing.

"Is that what this is about...the orcas?"

"As if you would care."

"Try me."

Kathryn's answer was to spit in Nora's face. As she was wiping it away, for the second time since they'd arrived, Randall called her over to the computer.

"I found the operational clock. Whatever is happening, happens at daybreak."

Chapter Six

Randall loved academia. He felt at home on a college campus. His own alma mater was the first place he'd been able to completely relax and immerse himself in learning. As Nora drove, he studied the website for The University of Washington. UW pegged itself as one of the world's preeminent public universities. Founded in 1861, the campus covered over seven hundred acres and served fifty-four thousand students.

"They have a tab on their website for sustainability. There's a nature blog, green certification, you can even take *the pledge*—whatever that is."

"Those things aren't bad in and of themselves, Randall."

"I know that."

"Do you recycle?"

"I'm not home enough to recycle. I'm barely home enough to pay the rent, and I didn't say sustainability was bad."

"You didn't say it, but your tone..."

He snapped the cover closed on the tablet. "You have to admit that a good percentage of the cyber attacks taking place are committed by militant environmentalists."

"That would be an excellent topic for a paper. Why don't you submit one to the director?"

"Why are you defending them?"

"I'm not defending them." She pulled into a visitor parking place in front of the building which housed Marine and Environmental Affairs. "There are people who are generally concerned about our environment, and I respect that. What I can't abide is when their methods put other people in danger. That's not acceptable. That's not how we do things here."

"Well, I have a feeling Professor Dresden is not one of the good guys."

"On that, we agree."

Randall had found the professor's schedule online. She had office hours from one to three, which meant she should be there. Unless she'd run already. He stood beside the rental car, bouncing on his toes. "How do you want to do this?"

"Take your backpack."

"Okay."

"I want you to wait outside her office."

"This gets better and better."

"You can hack into her computer?"

"Of course."

Giant trees paralleled the brick walk leading to the building. The sun was shining through the new shiny leaves, students were splayed out on the lawn— both alone and in groups, and the temperature was perfect. Hadn't he heard that Seattle was rainy all the time? Not today. Perhaps today was their day. Perhaps they'd break the professor's plan wide open and be home by sunset.

He doubted it, but a guy could dream.

Nora stopped short of the doors and pulled him to the side. "Walk me through it."

Which was so typically Nora that he had to smile. She didn't really understand the details of the cyber war they were fighting, but she could put the pieces together better than anyone he'd ever met.

"Think of it like a phone trace. As long as you keep the bad guys on the line, the good guys can run a trace."

"But not if they hang up."

"Correct."

"So I need to get Dresden on her computer."

"Or cell phone. Whichever she reaches for is fine. Once I get into one, I can access the other based on what I find there."

"How can you do that?"

Randall shrugged. "Everyone accesses their work email from their phones now. In fact, studies show that we access 97% of the sites we use on our desktop, from our phone."

"How much time do you need?"

"As much as you can get me. Put your phone on silent, and I'll buzz you when I've found what I need."

"I'll also patch you in so you can hear the entire conversation."

Randall pulled an earpiece from his backpack and stuck it in his ear. "Ten-four, boss."

"We're going to work on your attitude when this is over."

"Uh-huh."

Dresden's secretary couldn't claim she was busy

or not in—the professor had an open door policy and they could plainly see her sitting there at her desk. In fact, she looked up and smiled slightly before her eyes narrowed in concern.

Nora stood in the doorway, introduced herself, and when Dresden had walked to them she handed over her credentials. If it rattled Dresden, Randall couldn't tell. The professor was a small woman, mid-fifties, freckled skin with long reddish hair braided down her back.

Dresden motioned toward the chairs in front of her desk. "You're both welcome to come in."

"Mr. Goodwin will wait outside." Nora held off until Randall walked out and took a seat, then she closed the professor's door.

He smiled at the receptionist and took a seat as Nora began to grill the professor. He'd ascertained since working with her that Nora had two interrogation styles. When she thought it was beneficial, she could be subtle and gently lead suspects to the corner they'd box themselves into. Then there was her other style, which more resembled a demolition expert with a very big sledgehammer.

"We know your plans to destroy the Lower Snake River dams."

"Perhaps you're confusing me with someone else."

"I rather doubt it. You do understand that you'll go to jail for the rest of your life."

"Those dams are a hazard to the wildlife. That water provides a lifeline to the Orca population, but of course I'm not admitting to anything."

"We also spoke with Jonathan Coleman."

"I don't believe I know that person."

"And Kathryn Waters..."

"Ah, Kathryn."

Randall heard the squeak of Dresden's chair as she leaned back. It took him three attempts to guess the password for the school's network. WashingtonBears? Their mascot? These people needed a new network director. Now that he was on the secure side, not the public one, he'd have quicker access to her data there once he managed to piggy-back onto her device.

"So you admit you know her?"

"Of course. Kathryn attends several of my classes."

"She's a high school student."

"Yes. Like most universities, we're accepting students at an increasingly younger age. There are advantages and disadvantages to that."

"How would you characterize your relationship with Kathryn?"

"I wouldn't go so far as to label it a relationship, though I pride myself in taking a personal interest in my students. Kathryn is...special...as I'm sure you realize if you've made her acquaintance."

"And her coding skills no doubt served you quite well."

Dresden actually laughed. It sent a chill down Randall's spine. Sometimes they dealt with people who were mentally or emotionally unbalanced. Other times the perps they apprehended struck Randall as callously evil. Dresden was quickly falling into the latter category.

"Kathryn and I share a passion for protecting the environment, if that's what you're insinuating."

"Can you tell me where you were three evenings

ago at approximately nine forty in the evening?"

There was a slight pause. He could practically hear Nora smile. "Feel free to check your cell phone's calendar if that'll help."

"Why should I?"

"Because you can either answer my questions here, now, or I can have the Department of Homeland Security pull you in, and you can provide your answers at their facility."

"My. You must be very important if you have that sort of pull."

Nora didn't rise to the bait. Of course she didn't.

The program Randall was accessing allowed him to see all mobile devices within a predetermined range. He'd set it to ten feet—so far all he saw was his, Nora's, and the receptionist's. Dresden's was there, but not active at the moment. She was apparently careful enough to turn it off when she wasn't using it.

There was a sigh, and then he heard her rustle in a bag. The dot turned green when she turned the cell phone on, and that was as good as a *GO* sign for Randall.

As Nora quizzed her on various dates—some relevant, others not so much—Randall downloaded her calendar, contacts, app activity including GPS, texts, and phone records. The director had managed to obtain a search warrant for the information. Nora could have simply demanded the phone, but they didn't want to just stop Dresden, they wanted to prevent whatever she had planned. To do that, they needed to give her a little rope.

The entire download took less than three minutes. He buzzed Nora to indicate he had all the information they needed. She quickly ended the

interrogation and strode out of the office, never
bothering to look back at Randall. She wanted Dresden
to believe they were a dysfunctional team. She wanted
Dresden to believe she still had a way out of this.

Randall smiled at the receptionist. "Have a good
day."

"You too." The girl must have been a student at
the university. She nodded toward the direction Nora
had gone. "That can't be too easy."

"No...easy isn't a word I'd use in regard to my job."

He jogged to catch up with her at the end of the
hall. She flashed him a smile, and they strode back out
into the sunshine. Five minutes later they were on the
road headed back to the hotel.

"Why the hotel?"

"Because you need sleep."

"I'm good—honest." Unfortunately, at the
mention of *sleep* he yawned.

"I need you at your best, Randall. Take a couple
of hours."

He glanced at the clock on the rental's dashboard.
Ten minutes after two. Then he looked back down at the
data he'd retrieved. He was almost disappointed it was
so easy to find. In fact, it made him a little suspicious.

"She rented a boat."

"A boat?"

"For tonight. Well, the rental agreement that's in
a hidden file in her email—"

"Not hidden well enough, apparently."

"It specifies that she has it for a period of twenty-
four hours beginning at six p.m. Even gives the location
of the boat and the code to get through the gate." He
glanced at Nora, as he attempted to stifle another yawn.

"Think this is a set-up?"

"I do not. If I had to pick one word to describe Samantha Dresden, it would be arrogant."

"She certainly didn't sound rattled by your interrogation, which I would have been. Anyone with an ounce of common sense would have been."

"I think Professor Dresden sees it more as a chess match, and she's quite certain it's a match she will win."

"So what's she going to do with the boat?"

"I have no idea, but we'll be there to see firsthand."

She punched the speaker phone on her mobile and told the device to call the director. He picked up on the second ring. She succinctly described the meeting, assured him Randall would forward everything he'd found, and outlined her plan.

All that was left was to wait until six p.m. Oh, and apparently Randall was supposed to take a nap, which at the moment didn't seem like a bad idea.

Chapter Seven

The boat was a thirty-one-foot Camano Troll with silver paint and the word *Tahlequah* on the side. Apparently Dresden didn't go in for subtlety. Perhaps she'd picked the boat specifically because it sported the name of the mother orca that had carried her dead calf more than a thousand miles.

Nora and Randall were ensconced inside an adjacent boat. Supposedly it wasn't for rent, but the man had readily taken the two hundred dollars when they told him they had no intention of taking it out on the water.

"Works for me." He pocketed the money, wished them a good night, and strolled off whistling.

Nora stared out at an evening sky quickly turning to midnight black. Fortunately they'd grabbed sandwiches before accessing the boat. Randall had woken from two hours of solid sleep proclaiming he could eat an orca. It was a terrible joke, but she'd laughed all the same.

Darkness lay over Puget Sound, and Nora's restlessness was reaching a peak. How could she be exhausted and impatient at the same time? She picked up the binoculars the owner had generously provided and peered through them as Randall tapped away on his tablet.

"Separate teams have been deployed to each dam." He rubbed at the back of his neck, then resumed pecking on the keyboard. "They are all on-site at this point and currently working to assess the point of compromise."

"Can they do that in time?"

"If not, they'll take the dams completely offline until they figure it out." Randall glanced up at her and smiled. "But those guys are pretty smart. Now that we know the *where*, the *how* shouldn't be so hard to ascertain."

"You sound confident."

"I'm feeling good about it," he admitted. "All except this."

"Don't like boats?"

"I don't like swimming in my clothes in the dark."

Nora stretched her neck to the left and right, attempting to relax the muscles. "Hopefully it won't come to that."

They had both changed into a fresh set of clothes. Randall's polo was a Fendi that cost more than five hundred dollars. The chino trousers were made by Altea and cost under three hundred. She knew those details because she'd asked. It never ceased to amaze her what Randall spent on clothes. She'd opted for her other pair of black pants and a gray button up blouse. Total cost was less than ninety bucks.

The local police as well as Homeland Security had been brought up to date, but they had orders from the director to remain well back from Dresden's boat. The professor was an extremist, but she was also quite intelligent. No one doubted that she had a backup plan if the current one was waylaid. Nora and Randall's job was to disable both.

"Any new activity on her live feed?"

"Nothing since the timer popped up an hour ago."

Randall had discovered the site by hacking through the back door of her work computer. Fortunately, they'd been able to do all that remotely. There was no reason for Dresden to suspect her plans had been compromised. What was as disconcerting as the live feed—though they were clueless as to what she was planning on recording—was the number of followers she had, which numbered in the tens of thousands.

"More to the point, what is Samantha Dresden planning and why on this boat?"

"I can't answer that, Randall. All I can say is, you got lucky finding the receipt for this boat in her email files."

"Lucky? Boss, I'm good. It's time for you to admit that."

"Duly noted." The boat was for sale for over a hundred grand. The twenty-four-hour rental was a mere five thousand. They'd checked, and UW didn't pay very well. Which made Nora wonder who was funding Dresden, something the folks back at headquarters were working on.

And why spend so much on a boat?

It seemed an odd choice for a radicalized environmentalist.

She squinted through the binoculars. It seemed to her that the sky was lightening. Glancing at her watch she saw that they had just under an hour until sunrise, less than sixty minutes until daybreak, and they still had no idea what was happening. She caught movement fifty feet to the east. "Here she comes."

Randall slapped the tablet's cover shut and tucked it into his backpack. He walked gingerly to the front of the boat, sat next to Nora, and picked up the second pair of binoculars.

"Shouldn't we just arrest her now?"

"We could, but she's not going to crack as easily as Kathryn." The petulant teen had morphed into a compliant young woman after Detective Lawson arrived—which was how they'd obtained Dresden's name. "Our visit to her office didn't change her plans. You said the receipt for the boat came in two days ago."

"True enough."

Apparently Kathryn had met Dresden through an online environmental class. The two had hit it off right away. Over the course of the next six months the professor had carefully groomed the young girl. Undoubtedly she'd checked Kathryn's school records and realized she had a genius on her hands—literally. Kathryn had already run into trouble for minor infractions such as redirecting big corporate websites to environmental causes and establishing her own WikiLeaks-type presence in Seattle. The juvenile courts had placed her on probation and ordered that she have no internet access. Dresden had taken care of that small problem by purchasing her a state-of-the-art hotspot.

The professor wasn't wasting any time. She hopped onto the *Tahlequah*, walked straight to the helm, and started up the engines.

"Let's go."

Randall wound his arms through his backpack and jogged after her. They jumped for the back of the boat as Dresden pulled away from the dock.

Nora's plan was to see where the woman was going, then intercept and neutralize any threat. That plan shattered when Randall tapped her on the shoulder and pointed to the galley. After confirming that Dresden was focused on piloting the boat, Nora followed him.

The C-shaped galley was equipped with a full, if small, kitchen. Nora could just make out a bathroom and stateroom past the galley, but she wasn't focused on that. Instead her eyes were locked on the stacks of C-4 explosives and the countdown clock displayed on the flat screen television.

"Same as the live feed I was watching," Randall whispered.

They had fifty-three minutes until daybreak.

Apparently they also had fifty-three minutes until Dresden blew her hundred thousand dollar boat to bits. She definitely wasn't planning on getting her deposit back for the rental. The question was, who and what did she plan to take with her.

క్ర

Randall had been trained to do a lot of things—diffusing bombs wasn't one of them. Their mission was always to intercept the cyber-terrorist. Often that job included hacking into systems and stopping their nefarious plans, like Dresden's scheme to disable the dams on the lower Snake River. She'd started that plan in the cyber realm but hoped to complete it in real life—IRL, as the kids liked to say.

But this?

This was C-4 explosives with multiple detonators. He didn't know where to begin. Sweat slipped down his face, as he lowered his backpack to the floor.

From where they were standing, there were two ways out. They waited as the boat picked up speed, each minute that ticked by causing Randall's heart rate to accelerate a little more. Nora pulled her weapon and signaled for him to go back the way they'd come. She moved toward the ladder which led to the fly bridge where Dresden remained at the helm station. They would come at the professor from both directions.

Randall pulled his weapon and crept around the back of the boat. He could just make out Dresden on the fly bridge. She was backlit by the night lights of dozens of cruise ships, still anchored in Puget Sound.

That was her plan.

She was going to take as many cruise ships with her as possible. But how did she expect to survive the blast? Or was this a suicide mission?

Nora signaled him from the fly bridge, and they both stepped out into the open at the same moment.

"No need to be stealthy about it. I know you're there." Dresden checked the readings on the display in front of her, set the navigation on automatic and turned to face them.

Randall's heart sank as he saw the rope tied around her waist. She bent to pick up the anchor that was tied to the other end and moved in one fluid step to the edge of the boat.

"Stop right there." Nora's voice was steady, calm, commanding.

Dresden only smiled. "Or what? You'll shoot? Frankly, Agent Brooks, I don't care."

"You don't have to do this," Nora said.

Normally Randall would be making his way around the back of the perp, but all that stretched behind Dresden was Puget Sound, then Bainbridge Island, beyond that Olympic National Park, and finally the Pacific Ocean.

She'd chosen the place of her last stand well.

"Has it occurred to you that maybe I want to do this?"

"Why? You could live to fight another day." Nora moved a step closer and Dresden clutched the anchor to her chest.

"People love a martyr. I can do more for Tahlequah with my death."

"No. You can't. People will forget you before the next news cycle."

"So I should, what? Let you arrest me?"

"Sure. Lots of people write books from prison. Yours could be a best seller. Tell the story of the orcas. Tell people why your cause matters."

"You're good, and so is your partner Randall Goodwin. Nice job hacking into my system, Mr. Goodwin. Of course I had an alarm set to warm me if someone managed to do that. I've been following your moves since you accessed Jonathan's computer."

"Why students?" Randall asked. It angered him to think that this woman with her rage and violence would use kids at a time when they were most vulnerable.

"They're the next generation. This world, this

fight, is theirs."

"It's your fight, and you were using them."

"We all use each other. That's part of the human condition."

"Put the anchor down," Nora tried again. "Let us take you back in."

"That's not going to happen. You stopped my attack on the dams, but these cruise ships we're surrounded by, these albatrosses that are the epitome of American influence and arrogance...I will destroy them." Quick as a whisper in the night, she turned and dropped into the dark waters of Puget Sound.

Randall moved to dive in after her.

Nora reached out, pulled him back. "She's gone. See what you can do with the explosives. I'll call the director."

The director patched them through to the bomb squad. Randall might have been able to disarm one, but Dresden had anticipated that. There simply wasn't enough time to disarm them all. Even worse, she'd pre-programmed her target position into the ship's navigation program and the engines were now idling as the boat sat in the middle of the cruise ships' docking area.

"I want both of you to get out of there, now." The director's voice came through clear and strong.

"You're breaking up." Nora reached over and muted her cell. "Forget the explosives. Can you hack into the navigation system?"

"I can try."

It took precious minutes for Randall to free the navigation system from Dresden's program. Nora immediately piloted the boat toward the deepest waters of Puget Sound. Only then did she unmute her phone. The numbers flashing on the explosives were now under four minutes.

"I need you to pull up the satellite feed and tell me when we're clear of any other craft."

No doubt the director had been following their progress and understood her plan. He responded immediately with coordinates and reiterated that he wanted them off the craft before it blew.

"Where does he expect us to go?"

Instead of answering, Nora focused her eyes on the horizon, which was now stained with pink. Daybreak had nearly arrived. They were almost out of time.

"Find a way for me to rig this throttle, Randall."

He rushed back down to the galley.

Two minutes and twenty-eight seconds.

He returned to her side with a bungee cord, and they wrapped it around the throttle, holding the boat's engine at its maximum speed.

"Let's go." Nora tossed him a life preserver.

As they ran toward the back of the boat, they both fastened the belts of the preservers and pulled the cord that would inflate them.

"Ready?"

"As I'll ever be."

The water was cold and dark as he plunged beneath the waves. Bobbing to the top, he spotted Nora and side-stroked toward her. They could hear the *Tahlequah's* engines, but the boat itself was now out of sight. Then the morning's peacefulness was shattered by the explosion. The waves hit them a few seconds later.

Once the waters had calmed, Nora nodded back toward Seattle. Morning was breaking over the city.

Instead of high-fiving her, Randall pulled her closer, as close as they could get while they were both wearing fluorescent life preservers. "That was close."

"Indeed it was."

"You think that rope around Dresden's waist was knotted?"

"Something tells me it might not have been, but that's a problem for another day."

The sound of a boat approaching rose over the thud of Randall's heartbeat. He'd wanted more excitement than sitting behind a computer, but as his granny liked to say, *be careful what you wish for*.

As they waved at the rescue boat, he realized that they couldn't possibly stop all the dangers facing America—cyber or otherwise. But today they'd succeeded in stopping one, and for now, that was good enough.

The End

ॐ

Author's Note

This book is dedicated to my sister, Pamela Lindman. We share a love of all things dystopian, whether it's movies, television, or books.

When I began writing this story, the world had not yet heard of Coronavirus (or COVID-19 as it has come to be known). I had no idea that cruise ships around the world were about to face unparalleled struggles, or that the people on them would be in danger. I didn't envision the tragedy that would unfold first in China and later in Seattle, then across the United States and finally throughout the world. And so this book is also dedicated to us--to this generation. May God defend and guide us.

My understanding of technological advances is less than complete; however, I am concerned about our growing dependence on technology, both personally and globally. This series is designed to raise awareness regarding that dependence as well as any corresponding vulnerability. If the subject interests you, I suggest you do some research. In my opinion, knowledge is a good thing.

As is always the case, I am grateful for my pre-readers, Kristy and Tracy. This story was also made better by Teresa, who served as editor, cover designer, and formatter. All three of you are awesome.

And finally ...always giving thanks to God the Father for everything, in the name of our Lord Jesus Christ (Ephesians 5:20).

Blessings,
Vannetta

High Noon

Cyber Division, Book 4

Dedicated to
Carol Lilly

While this novella is set against the real backdrop of Zion National Park, I have taken great liberty with the hike through Behunin Canyon. The characters, as well, are fictional. There is no intended resemblance between the characters in this book and any real persons. As with any work of fiction, I've taken license in some areas of research as a means of creating the necessary circumstances for my characters. My research was thorough; however, it would be impossible to be completely accurate in details and descriptions. Therefore, any inaccuracies portrayed in this book are completely due to fictional license.

Contents

"Then I heard something
like the voice of a great multitude
and like the sound of many waters
and like the sound of mighty peals of thunder,
saying,
Hallelujah! For the Lord our God, the Almighty,
reigns."
~Revelation 19:6

"Not until we are lost
do we begin to understand ourselves."
~Henry David Thoreau

∽

Chapter One

They landed in Las Vegas, Nevada just past midnight on June eighth, picked up the rental car, and grabbed a meal on the way out of town. Randall drove for an hour and a half, then woke Nora, who took them the rest of the way into Utah, then past St. George and Washington, skirting Red Cliffs National Conservation area. She woke Randall when they reached Springdale. She had the sense of mountains towering on both sides of them, but in the darkness there were only shadows piled one upon the other.

Pulling into an all-night service station, they gassed up and grabbed coffee that had been brewed hours before.

As they walked back out to their rental, Randall sipped the coffee. "Sure there's not any Starbucks here?"

"Do you see a Starbucks?"

"All I see is stars." Randall craned his neck as he raised his arms over his head, stretched and cracked his back.

Randall was African American, six-foot-four, and had the shape and physical bearing of a professional football player. Randall's father had enjoyed a successful NFL career, but Randall had gone a different direction. His near-genius IQ, coupled with his ability to read computer code as if it was his native language, had landed him a spot on the Agency's cyber squad, and as Nora's partner.

They were a good team, maybe because they were so different.

Randall had attended MIT. Nora received both of her degrees at Texas Tech.

Randall could do phenomenal things with a computer. Nora preferred chasing the perps who had dedicated their lives to cyber terrorism.

And while Randall was twenty-seven, muscular, and athletic, Nora had passed the ripe old age of thirty-eight. She had no misconceptions about being an athlete, and she didn't care about that. She only needed to be able to run fast enough to catch the bad guys—marathons weren't on her bucket list.

The town of Springdale was less than six hundred residents and located immediately outside the entrance to Zion National Park. Nora's boss, Director Anderson, had arranged for someone to meet them at Zion's visitor center. Ten minutes later they were standing in the empty parking area briefing Daryl Tillotson, a park map spread across the hood of his vehicle.

"Do you think we need to ask all visitors to vacate the park?" The man in charge was pale with small bifocals and thinning hair.

"Would that even be possible?" Nora asked.

"Probably not."

"Then stop worrying about it. The important thing is to keep everyone away from this area." She stabbed the park map with her finger, then turned to glance at Randall, who was leaning against their rental, studying the open tablet in his hands. "Are you still showing Behunin Canyon as his location?"

"That's what the data is telling me, boss." He glanced up at her, worry coloring his normally sunny expression. "Though data sometimes lies—or rather, misdirects."

"We'll deal with that when and if we have to." She turned back to the park's manager. "I don't want anyone near that canyon. Understood?"

"Sure. Yeah. I got the call from your...uh...boss. We've shut it down and there's a park ranger waiting there for you now."

Nora resisted the urge to shake the man. She'd specifically said no one was to be in the area, which included park rangers. Now she'd have to use precious moments to send the person packing when they reached the designated parking area.

The park manager seemed eager to be rid of them and get on with his day, or perhaps he planned to go back to bed. "Continue four point four miles up this road. You'll see the parking area on the left."

They followed the Virgin River as the sky began to lighten. The gorge cut from the river was as spectacular as the descriptions she'd read—sixteen miles long, up to two thousand feet deep, and at times thirty feet wide.

"Wow." Randall tapped his window. "I googled this place, but the internet does not do the real thing justice."

"And let that be a life lesson for you, Randall."

His face crinkled into a smile. "It's sweet how you look out for me, boss."

"I'm not your boss."

"Uh-huh." He gave her a once-over. "Nice digs you're wearing. Where'd you find them?"

"In the bottom of my closet, and I'm very proud that I can still fit into them since I haven't hiked in ten years." She threw him a sideways look. "I guess you ordered yours online?"

"As soon as we received the *go* on this mission. Had to express it to my apartment, and before you ask, it's all from REI and the total cost was just under a thousand bucks. Well, plus the cost of the pack and the shoes."

"Do you really care how you look to catch a terrorist?"

"Look your best, feel your best, out-perform every time."

"Let me guess...your mom said that."

"Yeah, when I talked to her on the phone two nights ago."

"They're proud of you, Randall. They told me so at the awards dinner last month."

"It took a while for Pop to come around. He wanted me to play ball, or at least coach. But now...I think he's starting to see how important what we do is."

"The last six weeks should have convinced him when nothing else could."

The country had experienced a virtual rainfall of cyber attacks. People were more than a little concerned, not to mention hopping mad that their business and leisure were constantly being interrupted. There were calls for everything from federal oversight and installation of a national network and firewall to more severe sentencing of convicted cyber criminals. It seemed America was waking up to their vulnerability, and no one liked what they saw.

Nora pulled onto the grassy shoulder to navigate around a Road Closed barricade then continued to the Grotto Shuttle stop. Behind it was a small parking area, obviously only for authorized vehicles. Nora turned the Jeep Cherokee into the parking area and pulled up alongside the national park truck. The man who stepped out of the vehicle reminded her of a young Sam Elliott—tall, thin, unmistakably western, and of course sporting a thick black mustache that was lightly peppered with gray to match his hair.

"Tom Anderson." He shook both their hands. "What's this about?"

"I'm Nora Brooks. This is my partner, Randall Goodwin. As far as what this is about, I'm afraid you don't have the clearance to know that."

"Yeah. We really can't say." Randall shrugged his shoulders, as if to say, *What can you do? Orders are orders.*

"You've confirmed that no hikers are on the trail?"

"I have." His voice was deep, rich, and held a note of amusement. "Tell me this isn't one of those film shooting situations."

"Do we look like a filming crew?"

"Can't say as you do, but then filming people all look different."

"We are with the federal government—"

"I hate when we close national parks—"

"As do I." Nora spoke the words as if each were a sentence, something she only did when her patience was about to snap.

"Parks are for the people, by the way, the same people you're saying can't access this canyon today—all so someone can get the backdrop just right for a movie."

Nora put her hands on her hips, stared at the ground, tried to count to ten and made it to two—usually she could at least force herself to four, but this guy was really getting on her last nerve.

The name sewn into his shirt said *Anderson*.

It was time to let Park Ranger Anderson know exactly where he stood and what he was required to do. She was not going to lose the perp they were chasing because a park ranger thought he knew better than she did.

◈

Randall wanted to warn the guy, but he was forging ahead so quickly there wasn't time. So instead, he took a step back so he wouldn't get hit by any of the flying debris about to escape from Nora.

"Sir. This is a matter of national emergency. It is not a filming expedition."

"Uh-huh. I've heard that before."

"Thank you for coming out to confirm that the trail is empty—"

"No cars, as you can see. And the transport buses don't start running for another thirty minutes, so trust me. No one's there."

"Unless they packed in last night and didn't come back out." Randall had opened his tablet and was assessing the director's program. A healthy red dot still blinked at him from somewhere down the trail.

"That would be highly unusual and dangerous.

There are no facilities on this trail, not to mention mountain lions and—"

"Mr. Anderson."

"Tom."

"Tom." Nora flashed him a smile that reminded Randall of a flash of lightning. The man should back up, or better yet, hightail it out of there. "We're done here. Thank you for doing what you were asked to do. We need this area vacated right now."

"Vacated?"

"Yeah."

"You want me to leave?"

"Yes. That's what vacated means. Agent Goodwin and I will take it from here."

"Look, Agent Brooks. I don't know who you are or what you're doing here, but this is an 8.5 mile-hike with a 2400-foot elevation gain. There are eight places that require you to rappel as much as 165 feet, not to mention this isn't the part of the park you want to enjoy on a June day. The temperature is predicted to top out over one hundred degrees this afternoon."

When Nora didn't as much as blink, Anderson pulled off his ranger hat and slapped it against his pants leg. "What kind of equipment do you have?"

"We have what we need."

"Really? Two 165-foot ropes, webbing harness, rappel device, and a helmet?"

Nora glanced at Randall.

He wasn't sure exactly how to answer. They had the supplies, but he suspected they lacked the know-how. Still, he understood what she wanted him to say. "We have all that stuff, boss. We're good to go."

"See? We're good to go."

"But you've never even been here. This is a technical canyon far off the beaten path. Do you know how many people I rescue here each year? I don't want you, or your partner, to be one of them."

"Your concern is duly noted. Have a good day, Ranger Anderson."

He turned toward his vehicle, and for a brief moment Randall hoped the man would actually leave. That hope was short-lived. Anderson turned back to them, resolve chiseled into his expression. "I can't do it."

"Excuse me?"

"Can't leave you here. You look like rookies to me."

"Rookies?" Nora's voice rose an octave. "Ranger Anderson, I need you to leave the area immediately, or..."

She stopped, apparently stumped, and glanced again at Randall, who could only shrug. He doubted the wisdom of jumping into the middle of their turf war.

"Or what?" Anderson stuck his thumbs in his belt.

Randall had only seen people stand in that posture in movies. This guy looked like he had just stepped off a Western set. Maybe that's why he was worried they were filming.

"Are you planning to arrest me? Because you seem to be alone, and the park manager has closed off this area. It'll take some time to get someone up here to put the cuffs on me...if that's what you're planning."

Anderson's concern was one thing. The towering slot canyons around them were another. Randall figured that perhaps it was time he added his voice to the logical side of the argument.

"Nora, could I talk to you a minute?" Randall jerked his head toward the back of their vehicle. Once Nora had joined him, he spilled his reservations. "I know our training included this sort of scenario..."

"It included every type of scenario."

"Agreed." Randall shuffled from his left foot to his right, then back again.

"Just say it."

"Okay. It's been a while since either one of us has done any rappelling."

"And?"

"We're allowed to access local authorities if it's in pursuit of—"

"I know our guidelines."

"Then I think this fits. He knows this canyon. He's an experienced hiker, and there isn't even a remote chance that he's in on this."

"How can you be sure of that?" Her expression didn't change at all, but her voice softened a little.

"Are you kidding me? This guy..." Randall looked around her at Anderson, who raised a hand and waved in acknowledgement. "He's the real deal. I'll bet my life on it."

"You may be doing just that."

"If he wants to come with us, let him. At least until we're certain we can handle the terrain."

She blew out a huge breath, nodded once, and walked back over to Anderson. "My partner thinks we might need you."

"I guess that means he's the brains of the group."

Which caused Randall to snort, because he kind of was. But he was also the first to admit that IQ didn't always translate to knowing what to do in the heat of an op. Nora had that corner solidly claimed.

"You want to come along for the ride? Fine, but you need to understand exactly what you're getting into. We're chasing a cyber terrorist who is planning an EMP attack."

"Electromagnetic pulse? How would a single person even be able to do that?"

"We have information that he is carrying a device capable of taking take down all electronics in the tri-state area." She stepped closer to the ranger, her voice lowering to a growl. "That means 9-1-1 call centers, power grids, telecommunications—just to name a few. This perpetrator is armed, and he is dangerous. It's our job to find and stop him and we have approximately..."

She glanced toward Randall.

"Six hours and twenty-two minutes."

"We have a short window to catch him."

Anderson didn't even hesitate. "Sounds like we should get started then."

Which relieved a worry that Randall didn't realize he'd been harboring. While the cliffs around them were beautiful, they were also intimidating. He had a feeling this was going to be completely different than any op they'd been on before. The question was whether they could rise to the occasion. As he'd told Nora, it seemed to him like their chances of success were better with Anderson.

~

Chapter Two

Five minutes later they'd retrieved all their gear and buckled into their packs.

Anderson stood frowning at Nora and Randall. "Your packs are wrong."

"No, they're not. They're U.S. government military grade, and they're fully equipped." Nora stood with her hands on her hips.

"Desert camouflage—woodland, if I'm not mistaken—which is fine if you're in the Middle East. Out here? You want a red pack like mine. Something that a rescue team can see if you fall into a ravine."

"Then we won't fall into any ravines."

"But..." Anderson cinched his pack up on his shoulders, dawning finally coloring his expression. "You think he'll shoot you."

"I have no doubt that he will, if he sees us before we see him."

"So red is like a flag in front of a bull."

"Exactly."

"Which means my pack is...all wrong."

Nora dropped her own pack, pawed through it,

and finally pulled out a length of camo netting. She walked closer to Anderson, motioned for him to turn around, and covered his pack with it, knotting the corners so it would fit snugly.

"Better?" he asked.

"Better than red."

"You two certainly came prepared."

"They've sent us on ops all over the country," Randall admitted as he closed the cover on his tablet. "If there's one thing we are, it's well equipped."

"Mind if I see that?" Anderson stepped closer to Randall, but looked to Nora for permission.

"Sure. Why not."

Randall set the tablet on the hood of the jeep and opened the cover, accessing the director's program. Jericho had been expanded in the last month to include a mobile app. Of course it didn't display all the available information—occasionally certain pieces of data would be for the director's eyes only.

"Here we are—three green dots."

"Green means..."

"Friendly."

"How does your program know I'm friendly?" Anderson looked at him with a deadpan stare, and Randall realized he'd underestimated the man. Old didn't necessarily mean out-of-touch.

"I marked you that way."

"And it must be satellite driven."

"Correct. Our perp is here." He pointed to a red dot.

"That's four, maybe five hours away if we set a good pace." He stared at the tablet, shaking his head. "I don't even want to know how you can track people out here."

"I wasn't planning on telling you." Randall returned the man's smile. At least he was smart enough not to ask.

"Here's my problem."

Nora had walked over to join them. Anderson glanced from Randall to her and then back at the tablet.

"Only twelve people a day are allowed on this trail. In the summer, we might have half that number. I'm here to log them in as they start, and I'm here to check them off as they leave."

All three of them stared at the red dot.

Nora stepped forward, peering at the dot, then turning to look at Anderson. "So either you didn't see him go in..."

"Not likely."

"Or he's been there since your last day off."

Anderson ran a hand up and down his jawline. "That's possible. I was off two days ago. The person who backs me up might not be as thorough."

"Jericho—that's the name of the program— tagged this individual..." Randall clicked and zoomed and repositioned a few boxes. "First sighted thirty-six hours ago. He might have been there longer, but we weren't looking for him then."

"There's no water or facilities on this trail." Anderson's eyebrows squished together. "If he's waiting up there, then he packed in whatever he needed, plus carried an EMP device?"

"They can be surprisingly small." Nora glanced toward the trailhead. "As for our perp, apparently he's the type that believes in being prepared."

She motioned for Anderson to take the lead.

Nora went next, and Randall brought up the rear.

The day had lightened, though the sun had yet to break the horizon. The trail began climbing almost immediately, then settled into switchbacks as they passed a sign that read *Refrigerator Canyon*. The coolness of the shade was a welcome respite, and it was only six thirty in the morning. Randall didn't want to think about what the day would feel like in four hours.

Best to keep his focus on the moment, and the trail, and how they were going to disable an EMP.

The trail began to climb again as a sign proclaimed they were entering *Walter's Wiggles*.

"Twenty-one switchbacks," Anderson explained.

They reached Scout's Lookout fairly quickly. The view was nothing less than remarkable. It occurred to Randall that many people came to this park in order to appreciate nature. Here he was chasing a terrorist, but he could still pause a moment and enjoy the view. And in some ways the magnificent terrain reminded him of what they were fighting for. Zion National Park was an iconic part of America as much as New York City or Panama Beach or the Big Sur.

"There's a chemical toilet twenty feet down that side trail if anyone needs it." Anderson stopped, pulled out his water bottle and motioned for them to do the same.

Nora crossed her arms, tapping her fingertips against her upper arms. "Staying hydrated isn't our biggest worry at the moment."

"Actually, it is. You become dehydrated and you'll trip or fall or pull one of us down with you, and none of those things will catch your guy."

Nora shook her head, but apparently deciding it was easier to agree than argue, she pulled out her bottle and drank a third of it.

"How many more of those do you have?"

"Enough for one liter every two hours of hiking."

"Nora's always prepared," Randall explained. "One of the many reasons they put her in charge."

"Enough chitchat. Let's get going."

Anderson led them to the left, and they passed a sign that read *West Rim Trail*. Randall tugged on Nora's arm, holding her back. "Something's bothering you other than Anderson. What is it?"

"If our perp's been there for two days, I can't figure out why. It's overkill. He could have snuck in during the middle of the night, made the ascent, and been in place in plenty of time."

"You can't rappel in the middle of the night, and there's no other way to where Jericho says he is."

"I'm sure there are other ways—dropped from a helicopter, maybe. I don't know. There's something we haven't thought of yet and that, more than anything else, is what's bothering me."

They'd been walking less than five minutes when they passed a sign pointing to the right that read *Angel's Landing*. Anderson stopped and cocked his head like a beagle that had heard the call of a bird. And then suddenly he turned, stared in the direction of Angel's Landing and began running, the morning stillness broken by the sound of their hiking boots beating the trail.

ↇ

Nora and Randall rushed to catch up with Anderson. By the time they reached his position, he was approaching a young man whose hands had been duct-taped behind his back. The guy was wearing jogging shorts, a muscle t-shirt, and running shoes. One glance told Nora his arms and legs were covered with insect bites and scratches.

Anderson knelt behind the young man and pulled his pocketknife to cut through the duct tape. Randall retrieved a full water bottle from his pack, and Nora pulled the tape off the guy's mouth.

Before he said a word, the young man grabbed the water bottle and upended it.

"Slow down," Anderson warned. "You'll vomit the entire thing and feel worse than you do now."

The man lowered the bottle, looked at the three of them, and wiped his mouth with the back of his hand. "I thought..." His voice was gravelly, and he unabashedly swiped at the tears streaming down his face.

"I thought I was going to die out here."

"Deep breath, then tell us how you ended up this way." Nora didn't consider herself a cold-hearted person, but she needed to find out what had happened, and then it was critical that they return to the trail as quickly as possible. The operational clock was ticking, and she sensed that things had just become exponentially more complicated. "Who did this to you, what did they look like, and when did it happen."

"Right." He ran his fingers through his hair, hands shaking from dehydration or adrenaline or maybe fear. He raised the bottle, glanced at Anderson, and took a small sip.

Anderson plopped on to the ground beside him.

"What's your name, son?"

"Mario. Mario Morelli."

That explained the red hair and sunburned skin. He'd attempted to stay in the shade, but from the sunburned status of his skin hadn't been entirely successful.

"Tell us what happened," Nora said again. "From the beginning."

"I was jogging the trail yesterday morning..."

Anderson was already shaking his head. "You didn't come in via the Grotto Shuttle stop."

"No. The other way." Mario hesitated, licked his lip.

To Nora he had the look of someone who knew they were about to land in trouble; but then, how much worse could it be than being bound and left to die on a remote trail in Zion National Park? Apparently Mario arrived at the same conclusion.

"I came from the east, from the river. I'd done it with some buddies in the spring, and I thought...I mean, I know it's technically not allowed, but..."

"Did you bring any supplies at all?" Anderson's face had turned an angry crimson as his eyes swept the area, plainly devoid of supplies.

"I did. I had a pack, first aid kit, water, everything. But he took them."

The hairs on the back of Nora's neck stood at alert. "Who? Who took them?"

"The person who did this. Did you think I tied myself up?" Mario struggled to his feet and hobbled back and forth, down the trail a few steps, then back toward them.

"Look at me, Mario." Nora stepped in front of him. "I know you're scared, and I know you've been through quite an ordeal. We're going to get you back to the ranger station. Okay? And no one is going to press charges for you going...off trail."

She glanced at Anderson as she said this. He scowled but nodded once in agreement.

"But it's important that we know what happened, and we don't have much time."

"I guess I surprised him."

"Who?" Randall asked as he pulled out his tablet. "Age, height, anything at all that you remember would be helpful."

"Same height as me, I guess—five eight. But wiry and strong. I'd guess in his late thirties or early forties. He had shoulder-length hair pulled back and...and some gray in it I guess."

"Nationality?" Randall was typing onto the tablet as Mario spoke.

"Not American, I don't think. He had darker skin, like European or something, and he had an accent. Not that he said much."

"What happened, Mario?" Nora was still standing in front of him, but now she reached for both of his shoulders and squeezed them gently. "We need to know exactly what happened."

"I turned my back for one second. I was about to take a selfie of myself and the view when he jumped me." Embarrassment colored his cheeks, but to Mario's credit, he pushed on. "I guess maybe he knocked me out. When I woke up, my pack and phone were gone and my wrists and ankles were taped together."

Nora glanced up, met Anderson's gaze. His eyes were widened in amazement at what he was hearing, and he continuously formed and released a fist with his right hand. In that brief moment she realized that in front of her was a man struggling with a new and vastly different view of his world, one that didn't add up and certainly didn't make sense.

So Nora did what came naturally to her. She took charge.

"Mario, I'm going to ask you to sit here and slowly drink that bottle of water. Once you keep it down, we'll see if you can handle a protein bar. Deal?"

"Yeah. I guess." The young man flopped on the ground, staring at the bottle in his hand as if it held answers he needed.

Nora motioned Randall and Anderson to join her ten feet away.

Randall joined them, but continued to stare at the tablet. When Nora brought the group to a halt—out of earshot but within eyesight of Mario—he focused their attention on the screen. "I input the description Mario gave us. Jericho cross-referenced criminals with a known cyber terrorism background against the details I gave it and in conjunction with individuals who could possibly be in the area at this time."

He scowled at the screen. "We got a hit."

Nora leaned closer.

Ivan Karvatsky.

Ukrainian.

Five foot, eight inches tall, one hundred sixty-five pounds.

Wanted for cyber crimes, including case numbers T478B22, T567A05, and T589M67.

Nora was familiar with all three cases, and it didn't make her feel any better about what or who they were dealing with. "Go show that picture to Mario.

Once you've confirmed this is our perp, forward the information to the Director."

She turned to Anderson, who was pulling out his phone.

"Put that up."

"What?"

"You can't use that, Anderson..."

"Call me Tom." He sighed wearily, then stuck the phone back in his shirt pocket and buttoned the pocket shut. "I'm pretty sure we're on a first-name basis now."

"Fine, Tom." She touched his shoulder, turned him away from Mario. "Karvatsky has the ability to intercept any calls you make on a regular phone. Only an encrypted satellite phone like Randall has is safe to use. You don't want to call for help on that device. It would be like—"

"Wearing a red backpack?" He attempted a self-deprecating smile. "Waving a red flag?"

"Exactly."

"As you can tell, I'm out of my depth in this situation. I came out here to get away from just this sort of thing."

"I'm not following."

Tom studied the vista and the trail that lead to Angel's Landing. "I signed up after the 9-11 attacks. Served four years in the Middle East. It's not something... not something I talk about. Took me years to banish the images and memories, but seeing the picture of that man...seeing what he did to Mario...brought it all back. The things that humans can do to one another, well it boggles the mind."

"I understand this is hard, but for me? It's just another day on the job. We've dealt with situations like this before. It's what we're trained to handle."

"An EMP device?"

"Yes?"

"Small enough for one man to backpack in with?"

"Yes. Small enough to fit into a suitcase. We know that such devices exist, and we have corroborated data that this man has one and intends to use it."

"And you've dealt with that before? Because I wasn't aware such a thing was even possible."

"We haven't dealt with an EMP before," Nora admitted. "Listen to me. Regardless of their specific method or their particular reason for carrying out an attack, there are certain components of every cyber attack that are the same. This isn't like other crimes. This is a crime against humanity, against the world. Trust me when I say that in many ways, this is no different than a dozen other ops that Randall and I have been on."

Tom took in a deep breath, then gave her a single quick nod.

"Tell me what you think we should do about Mario, and Randall will send the message via the director."

"He can't walk back, not in his weakened condition."

"All right, can he make it back if you walk with him?"

"Maybe...probably..."

"But what?"

"I'm not ready to turn tail and run. Have Agent Goodwin—Randall—call park headquarters, tell them it's an emergency rescue."

"We can't do that, Tom. We can't have Care Flight hovering overhead. We need to be more...subtle."

"Right. Right. Wouldn't want to get the paramedics—"

"Shot. We don't want to get them shot."

"But this Ukrainian guy...he's not here. Randall's computer shows that he's still three hours from here."

"His phone is three hours from here. The program doesn't track people. It tracks devices. That's why we didn't know Mario was here on this trail waiting to be rescued."

"Right. Okay." Tom's lips pressed together in a straight, firm line.

When he spoke again, Nora knew he'd accepted their position and changed to operational mode. He'd moved from doubt through denial and straight into acceptance. She had to respect the man for that. It wasn't every day that you came up against a maniacal terrorist.

"Have two rangers walk up. Tell them the location is at the intersection of the Behunin Trail and Angel's Landing."

"We accompany him to the crossing and leave him."

"With some supplies."

"It's a good plan." Nora turned to relay the information to Randall, when Tom tugged her arm.

"Why didn't Karvatsky just kill him?"

Nora considered being less than honest with her answer, but she sensed that Tom needed to know. More than that, if he was going with them, he deserved to know.

"A dead body would have drawn attention. How many animals do you have here that feed on carrion?"

"Quite a few—vultures, condors, hawks and

eagles, even coyotes."

"And someone would have noticed that."

"Yeah. We would have hoped it was a deer, but we're obligated to check it out, especially if the location appeared to be on or near a trail."

"Karvatsky knew that. By binding Mario's hands and feet, and taking away his supplies, he insured that Mario wouldn't go anywhere."

"And he delayed Mario's death."

"Long enough for Karvatsky to do what he needed to and get out of the area. Either way, Mario would be dead and unable to identify him. But the way he did it, he managed to delay Mario's death, which helped increase the likelihood of Karvatsky's success as well as escape."

"What kind of person—"

"A ruthless one. The same kind of person who's working to bring down the grid across America."

Tom covered his mouth with his hand, worked his moustache down, then seemed to make up his mind. He stood straighter and hitched up his pack. "You tried to warn me, but I didn't listen."

"If you want out now, no one will judge you."

"I don't want out, Agent Brooks."

"Nora. First name basis, remember?"

"Fine. I don't want out, Nora. What I want is to help you catch this guy."

Thirty minutes later, Randall had relayed the message, they'd set Mario up at the junction of the two trails with supplies, and were on their way.

They had less than five hours to find and disarm a Ukrainian terrorist.

Chapter Three

"Rappelling can be the most dangerous part of climbing. It doesn't have to be. With adequate gear and correct form, it can be a safe and enjoyable form of recreation. Bad gear...incorrect form...and you risk being injured or killed." Tom waited to make sure he had their attention, then he pulled ropes, several carabiners, a harness, and a helmet from his pack.

Nora and Randall did the same.

Whoever had supplied their packs apparently knew what they'd need, because their equipment was nearly identical to Tom's.

"Basically, you use friction for a controlled descent." Tom demonstrated how to rig their rope to the anchor at their feet with a double-rope system.

What he was saying sounded familiar, and Randall remembered standing at the climbing wall during their training exercise going through a similar process. So why was his heart racing and his hands sweaty?

The first rappel was an easy backwards walk down a ninety-five-foot wall. That first moment of stepping off, leaning backwards into the harness and hanging in the air...it was something he wouldn't forget. It was also completely different from what they'd done on the rock wall at the agency. There was no net or padded mat to greet them at the bottom if they fell. There was no soft place to land.

Once at the bottom, Tom explained, "A single-rope system is a little easier, a little faster even...but you leave the rope fixed to the anchor and re-climb later to retrieve it."

"Not sure we'll be coming back this way." Nora actually looked in her element—she was breathing deeply and smiling.

How was that even possible?

She didn't rock climb for a hobby.

She didn't have any hobbies that Randall was aware of.

"A double rope system allows us to retrieve our line by pulling on one side of the rope." Tom demonstrated as he spoke. When he tugged on one side of the line, it caused the other side to snake up and through the anchor.

The second rappel was nearly twice the height of the first, and their rope anchored around a large ponderosa pine.

"Everyone having fun?" Tom asked.

"I can't believe you do this for a living." Nora adjusted her helmet, then went over the lip and straight down a one hundred fifty-foot drop.

"Actually, it's kind of cool," Randall admitted. "Beats chasing the bad guys on the internet."

He followed Nora, his mind flashing back to Mario Morelli, a twenty-six-year-old kid left to die in

Zion National Park. He'd love a few minutes alone with Ivan Karvatsky once they found him. He slapped the wall to slow his descent and landed softly on his feet next to Nora.

"You okay?"

"Sure thing, boss. Just taking my frustration out on this rock face."

"Hey." She waited until he looked directly at her. "Good call on bringing Tom along."

"Did someone say my name?" Tom landed beside them, unclipped his rope, and pulled it down.

"Nora and I were discussing what a great tour guide you are."

"Glad to hear it." He nodded toward the edge. "We're still a hundred and ten feet above the canyon floor. This time we rappel off two bolts near the edge."

"Why are we going down again?" Randall shook his head in confusion. "Wouldn't our Ukrainian friend want to be at a high point to set off his rocket or EMP device or whatever he's carrying?"

"They've picked the best spot for operational overlap." Nora turned in a circle, hands on her hips. "You can bet they've thought this one out. It's not just how high you are. It's where you are. Think Venn diagram and overlapping circles."

"We can put up the ropes after this, at least for a little while." Tom wiped his arm across his forehead. The temperature had risen considerably, and it was only half past eight in the morning. "Once we cross the canyon, there's three more rappels totaling four hundred feet."

"I can hardly wait." If Nora was uncomfortable with their current position, she was hiding it well, but then Randall had never seen Nora in a situation she couldn't adapt to.

Top of Reunion Tower.

Middle of Puget Sound.

Chicago, New York, even a nightclub in Miami.

They'd always gone where they needed to go and done what needed to be done. Rappelling down a rock face wall wasn't going to stop her.

The director's update had not brought any good news. If anything, the situation was worse than it had been when they arrived at Zion National Park.

Jericho had upgraded the possibility of a major coordinated EMP attack to 89%.

Randall clipped his carabiner to the rope, tugged once to confirm the hold was solid, and followed Nora over the edge.

When Tom joined them at the bottom, they packed up the ropes. Each drank a third of a liter and consumed a protein bar.

"We made up a little time on that section." Randall studied the tablet, somewhat surprised it still showed a solid signal. That was the cool thing about satellite devices. They really did work almost anywhere. "Two hours and forty-five minutes until high noon."

"Someone bring along Gary Cooper's movie?" Tom asked.

"Yeah, and Nora packed popcorn too."

"High Noon is the mission name," Nora explained. "From what data we've managed to intercept, that's also the time of the attack."

"Why noon?"

"Why not? It's when the highest number of people are at work, taking a lunch break, picking up the dry cleaning..."

"Not here," Tom pointed out.

Nora glanced at Randall. He nodded in tacit agreement. Tom was in this operation now. He deserved to know the truth.

"There are a dozen EMP attacks planned, if our intel is good, and it usually is. Randall and I were sent to stop this one, because it may be the largest."

"Largest?"

"It appears to have the biggest range as far as destruction."

"Destruction...you mean..." Tom stopped, unable to find or voice the words.

"I'll be honest with you, Tom. We don't know. If it's a non-nuclear electromagnet pulse, then there will only be damage to devices and the grid. On the other hand, if it's a nuclear device and depending on how high of an altitude they're able to achieve..."

"Yeah. Okay. I get the picture."

"If you want out, we certainly won't judge you. There's time to put some distance between yourself and whatever Karvatsky has planned."

"Leave you two out here alone? And miss all the fun? Not going to happen." His cheerful façade slipped, and Randall saw a determination in the man that he hadn't noticed before. "This Karvatsky left another man to die in my canyon. I'd like to be there when you apprehend him."

"There's another reason Karvatsky might have picked midday—the stock market is still open." Randall slapped the cover shut on the tablet. It was heavier than what he usually carried, since it was a hardened cover which would supposedly withstand an EMP. Randall hoped they didn't have to test that. "Cyber bugs love to mess with the stock market."

"It's possible you two have been doing this too long." Tom pulled his hat off and resettled it on his head. "You're entirely too nonchalant about things."

"You never get used to it," Nora admitted. "But you learn to deal."

The open canyon had a sandy bottom. They picked their way around several large, unusual potholes.

"Our next rappel is only ninety feet, going into a slot canyon. Like before, there are two bolts on the right in the rock floor..."

"I hear a *but* coming." Randall had been peering down into one of the potholes. Now he jogged to catch up with Nora and Tom, who had stopped well short of the edge.

"The rappel itself is straightforward, but over the years, several people have fallen. They misjudge how steep the slab is."

"Let's not misjudge then."

Again, Nora went first.

Randall peered down at her. They were repelling into a narrow stretch of canyon. It was beautiful, and it also looked like the perfect spot for an ambush.

"You okay?" Tom waited, watching him, and probably misinterpreting his hesitation.

"Yeah. I'm good." He went over the edge. He was halfway down, had glanced first down at Nora, then up at Tom who was peering over the edge, when he looked to the right and saw something shiny. He grasped a rock in that direction and snatched at a necklace that someone had probably lost long ago. Stuffing it into his shirt pocket, he pushed off gently, swinging left and down.

At the exact moment he pushed into that swing, three things happened at once—so close together as to seem almost simultaneous.

He felt a sudden, searing pain in his left arm.

The crack of a rifle shattered the canyon's silence.

And Nora shouted for everyone to "Get down."

All of those things seemed to happen at once, though of course they didn't. Split seconds separated the perp pulling the trigger, the bullet ripping through Randall's arm, and Nora's shout of caution.

One part of Randall's mind understood what had happened.

Another part insisted that perhaps he'd managed to impale himself on a sharp rock. Then the perp fired again, and he understood fully that they were under attack.

༄

Nora knew she was completely exposed, but there was no way she was letting go of Randall's rope. He didn't need her to rappel down, or he wouldn't if he had two good arms, but even from where she was standing, she could see the blood seeping through his sleeve.

Tom peeked over the top of the ledge, pointed to his eyes with two fingers, then to the north with one. She gave him a thumbs-up.

But now she had a real dilemma. Leave Randall and take off after the perp? Or stay and risk both of them being shot by the creep? She decided to put faith in Randall's common sense, training, and athletic ability.

She took off after the perp.

Due to the narrowness of the canyon, she could only see a few feet ahead. She opted to keep her back against the opposite canyon wall, since that was the only direction Karvatsky could have shot from. Nora pulled her weapon, chambered a round, and began creeping through the narrow canyon. Small pools of water glistened on the canyon floor. The walls were so close together she could have reached out and touched the opposite side.

The occasional hardy tree sprouted out of the rock, forcing her to duck down or lean out. She chose to duck.

She continued a little over a quarter of a mile, and then the trail turned down a narrow, 50-foot chute into a lower section of the canyon. She didn't like the looks of it. Too easy to get ambushed again, which wouldn't help Randall at all.

And suddenly she needed to know Randall was okay. She holstered her weapon and jogged back to where she'd left him. Randall was propped up against the opposite wall of the canyon from where he'd rappelled. Tom had pulled out his first aid kit and was applying a pressure dressing to Randall's upper arm.

"How bad?"

"Through and through. Tore through some muscle, but missed the bone. He's lucky."

"I'm lucky. That's the funniest thing I've heard all day." Sweat dripped off Randall's forehead, but he offered a smile. "Help a guy out and fetch my pack?"

Nora ignored the request, though she took it as a good sign that he was still focused on the mission. Instead, she turned to Tom. "How did you get him down?"

Tom grunted as he checked the dressing, then began to wrap the arm. "Randall managed to rappel with one arm and his feet, something I have never seen before."

"Yeah. He's always been an overachiever."

"Thanks, boss."

"You got it, Randall."

Their eyes met, and Nora felt a lump in her throat. Why couldn't it have been her? This man had too much of his life in front of him to be killed now. Her resolve to see this through and see them safely home hardened as she accepted for the first time how much she'd come to care for her partner.

"You getting sentimental on me, boss?"

"Stop calling me that."

Tom finished with the wrap and picked up the bloody compresses, bandage package, and a good length of Randall's sleeve that he'd cut to access the wound. He stuffed it into a small trash bag and zipped the bag into a separate pocket in his pack.

"You let him cut your shirt?" A smile played across her lips in spite of her worry.

"He didn't ask."

"It's new."

"And from REI—the very best of active wear."

"Not to mention based on what you told me earlier, I'm estimating it cost around two hundred dollars."

"Maybe the agency will reimburse me."

Tom shook his head. "You two are something else." He repacked the first aid kit, then offered Randall a bottle of water and two pills for the pain.

"Morphine?"

"Tylenol. Wouldn't want your reactions impaired."

Nora fetched Randall's pack and handed him the tablet, which he opened, accessed his program, and then stared at in surprise before tapping more keys.

"So, he's the tech side of the team."

"He is. MIT-certified and everything."

"No sign of Karvatsky when you went up canyon?"

"No. But you saw him?"

"I saw someone...he was using a rifle with a scope, which explains how he made the shot from that distance."

"Why didn't he kill me?" Randall continued working on the tablet, but he sounded genuinely curious.

Tom plopped onto the ground and took a swig from his water bottle. "I think he tried."

"You moved, Randall. Remember?" Nora replayed what had happened in her mind. "I was looking up and saw you move to the right, hesitate, then move back left."

"Oh, yeah." He reached into his pocket and pulled out a pendant on a silver chain.

Tom took it from his hand. "We find stuff like this all the time. Maybe it gets snagged and someone doesn't realize they've lost it. Maybe it gets dropped from above."

"What is it?" Nora asked, as goose bumps cascaded down her arm.

"St. Francis of Assisi, patron saint of animals."

"Hmmm. Well, if that's a sign, I don't get it."

Tom handed it back to Randall. "That pendant might have saved your life. You might want to keep it. As for St. Francis, I think one of his most popular sayings applies here."

"I'm all ears." Nora regretted the cynicism in her voice. She was trying to get back on emotional solid ground. She'd humor Tom while they were resting, while they figured out what to do with Randall, then she planned to capture or, if the situation warranted, kill Ivan Karvatsky.

"Let's see if I can remember this right." Tom recapped his bottle and pushed it into an outer pocket of his pack, then adjusted the camouflage netting. "*Start by doing what's necessary; then do what's possible, and suddenly you are doing the impossible.*"

His eyes met hers, and Nora was suddenly back on an Amish farm in Indiana. She'd been chasing a cyber punk then, too. The op had resulted in her partner being killed. And the time with Benjamin Lapp had caused Nora to think about the spiritual side of her life—which she hadn't been apt to do before that.

"Are you a believer, Tom?"

"I am."

"Huh."

"You're not?"

"Verdict's still out."

"That's okay. I've heard that God is a patient fellow."

Yeah. He reminded her of Benjamin Lapp a lot—that same calm certainty. What must that feel like?

Randall had been typing with only his right hand, which wasn't a problem since he was right-handed, but it had slowed him down a bit. Not to mention the pain was probably messing with his concentration. But now he cleared his throat. "You guys need to look at this."

Nora and Tom sat on each side of him, and together the three went over the video three times.

There was no denying what was on the screen. Randall had backed up the video that was focused on Karvatsky's position, or what had been his position for the last eighteen hours. As they watched the single red dot split into two, one moved toward their position, and then rejoined the first.

They weren't dealing only with Ivan Karvatsky.

There were two different terrorists...at least.

Which changed everything.

Chapter Four

Randall sat staring at the opposite wall of the slot canyon as Nora and Tom argued about the best way to proceed.

Nora absolutely refused to leave her partner.

"There's no way he can do four more rappels," Tom argued. "Not with the injury to that arm."

"He did it before. He can do it again."

"The bleeding will increase if he tries, not to mention he's bound to be weaker from the pain and loss of blood."

Randall cleared his throat, and they both turned to look at him. "Do I even have a say in this?"

"Of course you do." Nora looked agitated and ready to go. "But I'm telling you that staying here on your own is more dangerous than going with us."

"And I'm reminding you both that I'm the only one with medic training here. We're lucky to have stopped the bleeding. If Randall tears it open further..."

Randall held up a hand, cutting off their explanations. "I'm going. As far as I can, anyway."

Which seemed to settle it. They'd take it one

wall at a time. Tom led them to the right side of the slot canyon, accessed a small trail up into the woods, and stopped in front of a ponderosa near the edge.

"How did he get up to where we were?"

"What?" Tom and Nora turned to stare at Randall simultaneously.

"How did Karvatsky, or his sidekick, get up to where we were? Climbing up these rock faces has to be harder than rappelling down."

"It definitely takes more skill and experience," Tom said. "People do it, but not often, and not in the heat of summer."

"And why now? Why when we were halfway to him? Did he have some sort of perimeter trip wire or—"

"He had a monitor on Mario." Nora closed her eyes for a moment. "It's the only explanation that makes sense because once he's alerted that we're on the trail, it still takes some time to catch up with us. As you said, climbing up is twice as hard."

Randall knew she was beating herself up for not anticipating Karvatsky's every move, but there was no way they could stay continually ahead of a perp. It was the nature of the job that they spent the majority of their time reacting and playing catch-up.

"Okay. Say he had a monitor on Mario. That monitor triggered a warning to let him know that Mario had moved."

"And he certainly didn't move on his own," Tom pointed out.

"So Karvatsky sends his drone to check it out."

"Halfway there, the drone picks up our images." Randall picked up the narrative. "He sends his sidekick to intercept us at the slot canyon, figures it's the best chance he'll get, and takes his shot."

"It was a good spot," Nora admitted.

"His drone must be state-of-the-art because we never heard or saw it."

"We have a drone." Nora nodded toward Randall's pack. "Maybe it's time we use it. Tom, how close are we? And how difficult are the rappels?"

"This drop is seventy feet. From the bottom you have a pretty good view to the north, though we'll continue south. Rappel 7 is ninety feet, and a more complex two-stage endeavor. The final is what we call The Big Exit—150 feet off two bolts. It also requires you to step off several outcroppings before going vertical."

Randall knew what he wanted to do. "Help me find a way down this cliff, and I'll set up a surveillance position at the bottom. We'll send the drone out and decide the best way to proceed from there."

Tom began to remove his supplies, but Nora stopped him with the shake of a head. "Your ropes and your harness are all brightly colored..."

"Which is common for climbing, sort of like wearing a bright orange hunting vest."

"But in this case, we're the hunted. Your supplies stay packed. We use the camo harness and ropes that we brought. We need every advantage we can find."

Randall found it interesting watching Nora and Tom negotiate. She'd accepted him as a full member of the team for two reasons.

They needed his help.

And she trusted him.

For Nora, things were simple like that. It was something he was still learning. Nora and Tom helped Randall into the harness, then basically lowered him down the seventy-foot wall. Fortunately the pool he landed in was nearly dry. Five minutes later, they were kneeling beside him as he released and directed the drone.

"Why didn't we use this sooner?" Tom asked.

"Someone who knows what to look for can detect a drone fairly easily. We'd rather keep the perp completely unaware that we're on his tail."

"But since Karvatsky already knows we're coming—"

"He knows someone is coming," Nora pointed out. "He most certainly knows there are two of us, but that doesn't mean he knows about you, Tom. A drone is no different from a camera. It can't take in the entire field of view, only what its lens is focused at. I was already at the bottom and Randall was closer to the bottom than the top when he was shot, so more than likely the drone picked up me and Randall, but not you."

"All right. That's good then. We outnumber them, and they might not know it."

"Also, they might predict that I'd go back with Randall. Obviously they know they hit him. I'd say there's a fifty-fifty chance they won't be expecting us."

"Won't they just send their drone out again?"

"Doubtful," Nora said. "Drones have a limited range and have to be recharged frequently. I don't think they've had time to get it back up."

Randall had already considered the possibility that they had more than one drone, but there was only so much a person could pack into a remote location. Plus, drones of that caliber weren't cheap. He was betting their lives that Karvatsky only had the one. "Fortunately our drone is probably better than theirs, and now it looks like we have contact."

They crowded around the small screen as Randall clicked and zoomed. Suddenly they were looking at Ivan Karvatsky and another, shorter man who could have been his brother—the resolution was that clear. They could actually make out the similarities in their profiles.

Which was the good news.

The bad news? Karvatsky had set up a small rocket on a launch pad. When Randall zoomed in, they could just make out the countdown clock. They had forty-three minutes.

§

Their supplies contained an extra pair of communication buds. Nora showed Tom how to use them, then turned to Randall.

"Ready?"

"I am."

"There's plenty of time remaining on the drone?"

"Two hours, though..." He hesitated, then voiced the concern they both knew was one of many weaknesses in their plan. "If he manages to set off that EMP, it'll fry the drone."

"Then we won't let him set it off." She reached down to her ankle holster and pulled out her back-up weapon—a Sig Sauer P320. "Do you know how to use this?"

"I do." Tom pulled the slide, confirmed the barrel was empty, then popped out the magazine.

"It's full. You have fifteen rounds. Let's hope you don't need them all. And keep one in the chamber. If it comes down to it, when it comes down to it, every second will count."

She squatted down in front of Randall. The bandage around his arm continued to seep blood, though it looked to be at a reduced rate. The compress was doing what it was supposed to and helping the wound to clot. Unfortunately, the walk and the climb down had opened some of it up again. She wished they had time to rewrap it, but if Karvatsky had a nuclear EMP device and was allowed to set it off, then it wouldn't matter if Randall's arm was bleeding. "I'll be back for you, Randall."

"I know you will, boss."

He gave her that cocky smile that he'd been giving her since he was first assigned as her partner, and perhaps that was what caused Nora to do something completely contrary to her nature. She put her hand on the back of Randall's head, pulled him toward her, and rested her forehead against his. She breathed in his scent and thanked the God that Tom and her old friend Benjamin Lapp believed in for his friendship.

Randall reached into his pocket and pulled out the Saint Francis pendant. "Take this. It was good luck for me."

She put the chain over her head and tucked the pendant into her shirt, could feel it there next to her heart. "I'll give it back to you when this is over." Then she ruffed his hair, stood, and said to Tom, "Let's go."

She might have enjoyed the next rappel under different circumstances. The first drop landed them near another dry pool. For the second drop Tom led her down canyon, where they rappelled down a smooth wall and landed on the other side of a pool with a good amount of water remaining in it. They were able to avoid the pool by walking on a narrow shelf above the water. Then the canyon once again turned sandy as they approached the mouth. They scrambled over several large boulders, and suddenly they were at the final two rappels, which was really one long plunge totaling 320 feet.

She stopped a few feet shy of the edge and dropped to her stomach. Tom did the same.

"How are we doing, Randall?"

"Their attention is still focused on the rocket."

"Have you been able to determine what type of EMP it is?"

"Negative, but I sent a screen shot to Jericho. Awaiting results."

"The time clock..."

"Twenty-four minutes."

"Roger that."

She clicked off, crawled to the edge and peered over, surprised that Tom followed. From their height, she was treated to an excellent view of red and tan sandstone walls that stretched off into the distance. It would be easy to get lost out there. It would also be easy to sneak in, which was no doubt what Karvatsky had done. She understood now that he hadn't originally rappelled down as they had. There was no way he could have carried such heavy equipment. Besides the rocket itself, there was a launch pad, a tent with camping gear, even a cook stove.

"He must have set up days ago," Tom muttered.

It was a big drop, but far enough away that there wasn't a chance either of the perps could hear them. Nora could now understand why Karvatsky had picked the spot. Basically he was able to launch the rocket out and over the plateau. The question was how high his rocket would go and what type of EMP he was using.

If it was nuclear, and they didn't stop him, it would kill everyone in the surrounding area. Even as that thought passed through her mind she was grateful he'd picked a sparsely populated position.

But of course Karvatsky wasn't an altruistic person. Saving lives hadn't figured into his choice of location. She could practically see the overlapping circles of his and the other eleven devices. Infrastructure throughout the entire southwest would be obliterated... California, Nevada, Utah, Arizona, and New Mexico would all be offline. Everything from 9-1-1 call centers to electrical grids would be defunct.

She belly-crawled backwards and stood once they were both well clear of the cliff. "Describe the descent to me."

"The first rappel is one hundred and fifty feet. There are several outcroppings you have to step over, and past that is a landing zone. You can't see it until you get there. From the shelf, you can scramble into a small alcove—"

"A cave?"

"Of sorts. It's small."

"Would we both fit?"

"Yeah. I think so."

"All right. I go first. You follow. If there's any indication that they see us, you do not join me. Understand? You go back to Randall. He'll call in reinforcements to get you out of here."

"If there's time."

"Correct."

"Better case scenario...we both make it to the cave."

"Once there, we reassess. If nothing has changed, we do the final rappel—"

"One hundred and seventy feet. Twenty feet of back walking, then you're free hanging."

"We do it together. You'll take up a position behind the large boulder to the south and provide cover fire. Try to draw them away from the EMP device, and I'll attempt to disable it."

If he was hesitant about her plan, he didn't show it. Or maybe he just didn't have a better idea. "I'm in," he said.

"Thank you." She keyed her microphone and relayed the plan to Randall, and then she was dropping off another cliff—only this time, her main goal was to be completely silent.

Chapter Five

Randall had the drone focused in on Team Karvatsky. Both men were now concentrating on the small rocket atop the launch pad. Karvatsky held a tablet and was apparently running through a checklist.

Randall noticed movement against the rock face behind Karvatsky. He split the screen into two views and zoomed one side in to better see Nora and Tom.

"I have you on descent and can confirm no one is looking your way."

As he watched, first Nora then Tom disappeared into the cave. Karvatsky was waving his arm and apparently berating the other man, though it was impossible to say. If only he had audio...

Nora and Tom stepped out of the cave and began to rappel into the final drop. They must have been midway down when something happened—Randall didn't see what.

Perhaps a small pebble slipped down the rock face.

Maybe the sound bounced off the canyon wall.

Or it could have been that Karvatsky randomly

picked that moment to look back and over his shoulder.

"Freeze in place." He kept his voice low, measured, calm—though he felt none of that. If Karvatsky could see them, if he took a shot now, Nora and Tom didn't stand a chance.

But could he see them?

Randall wouldn't have been able to pick them out if he hadn't been watching their descent from a slightly higher elevation. Their camo clothing, packs and rope blended in almost perfectly with the rock face.

Almost perfectly.

But would that be good enough?

"Continue to hold."

Now Karvatsky and the other man were both watching the rock face, searching it for what they felt but couldn't see.

Then something on the tablet beeped. Karvatsky turned his attention back to the screen and stared down at the device, touching buttons and again gesturing with his free hand. And then they both turned away from the rock face. Randall zoomed in and saw what the commotion was about. The timer had counted down to the two-minute warning.

"Proceed with caution. Time of detonation now one minute fifty-eight."

Nora and Tom dropped to the ground in one swift descent. Their movements were as coordinated as any Broadway dance group. As Randall watched, Tom sprang to a nearby boulder and pulled his weapon while Nora crept closer to Karvatsky and the rocket.

"The tablet is controlling the rocket, Nora. Get the tablet that Karvatsky is holding."

And then she was running toward the perps,

and Tom was laying down cover fire. Karvatsky and his man turned at the same time, but only the second man pulled his gun. Karvatsky's attention immediately jumped back to the tablet in his hands, impervious to the chaos erupting around him.

ॐ

Nora had never felt so terrified in all of her career, in all of her life, as when she was dangling from the rope and Randall said "freeze."

She felt her heartbeat thrum against her chest.

Sweat beaded along her forehead, her back, even her hands inside her gloves.

She had the irrational fear that a drop of sweat would splash to the floor of the canyon and reveal her position.

And in that moment, she became aware of the pendant Randall had given her, resting against her heart. St. Francis of Assisi.

Start by doing what's necessary.

Then do what's possible.

And suddenly you are doing the impossible.

She didn't know if she believed that a pendant could save someone's life. She didn't know where she stood on saints. But she did realize in that moment that she believed in God, that somehow Tom had been sent when they needed him, that Randall had been spared, and that they could and would be able to do the impossible.

"Proceed with caution..."

She and Tom hit the ground simultaneously, making no more sound than a breath of wind on a beautiful June morning. Once Tom was in position and had pulled his weapon, Nora hit full speed as she sprinted toward Karvatsky and the rocket. There was no longer any pretense of moving stealthily. Tom was behind the boulder, shooting as soon as Karvatsky and his sidekick turned toward them.

And Nora?

Nora ran straight at Karvatsky.

She trusted that Tom would not shoot her, and Karvatsky's goon was trying to pull his weapon and leap for cover in the same moment. Karvatsky's eyes flicked up to her then back down at the tablet. Perhaps he was trying to accelerate the launch. Or maybe he was unprepared mentally for what was happening. More than one perp had lost to Nora because he'd never envisioned being beaten.

The tablet shook in his hand.

He took a step backwards.

He glanced up again, his eyes wide in disbelief.

No doubt, he was shocked to see a slight, middle-aged, red-haired woman running straight at him with her weapon drawn. That could be disconcerting for anyone.

Tom hit Karvatsky's guy, who shouted out and slumped to the ground. Nora was aware of that and even saw his movement in her peripheral vision. But her focus was on Karvatsky and she came to an abrupt stop, standing three feet in front of the man, her weapon drawn.

She could read the tablet upside down.

Fifty-four seconds.

"Drop it, or I'll shoot."

Karvatsky did exactly the wrong thing. Instead

of dropping the tablet, he took another step backwards, took a step towards the rocket that still rested on its launch pad.

Nora knew she didn't have time to negotiate.

She shot him point blank, center mass, and snatched the tablet from his hands as he fell to the ground.

"What now, Randall?"

"Shoot it."

"Say again."

"I don't know how to stop it, Nora. And I can't do it from here. Put the tablet on the ground and shoot it. If that's the actual controlling device, and not merely a monitor, it should stop the launch."

Tom was standing next to her now.

He took the tablet from Nora, set it on the ground five feet in front of her, and quickly returned to her side.

Nora raised her weapon and fired.

The tablet exploded into a myriad of pieces, the sound of her discharged firearm ricocheting off the canyon.

"What now?"

"I think you should run."

"Run?" Tom offered her a small, tight smile. "I don't know, Nora. I don't know what's going to happen, but based on what the countdown clock read...if it's still going we have approximately twenty-eight seconds."

Which they both knew meant running wouldn't make any difference if they truly were in danger. You can't outrun the fallout from a rocket.

She turned to Tom.

"Other guy?"

"Dead."

"Thanks for your help."

"Don't mention it."

They stood there, in the bright sunshine of high noon, and Nora found herself offering up a prayer to God, though she didn't understand how she knew to do that, if she was doing it correctly, or even if God worked that way.

But it felt right.

And a memory stirred from somewhere deep in her soul, of sitting with her grandmother, of folding her hands together, of her nana's voice in her ear.

Randall's voice came back through her comm unit. "I think we're clear."

"You think?"

"We're clear, Nora. It...we're well past the countdown clock. You stopped it."

Relief flooded Nora's body, and she became aware that she was incredibly thirsty. She turned to Tom and gave him a high-five, then squinted her eyes against the bright sun until she found Randall's drone. She offered a wave and a thumbs up as the tension coursing through her body drained away, the adrenaline surge evaporated, and her left arm began to shake.

If Tom noticed, he didn't mention it.

Shoulders touching, they turned and began the walk back toward the cliff wall. It was time to go and fetch her partner.

ॐ

Chapter Six

Three months later

Randall stood under the Double Arch at Arches National Park, gaping up at the fantastic structures created by the wind-blown sand. He hadn't really planned on coming back to Utah, but Nora had asked. When Nora asked, he found it difficult to say no.

She turned to smile at him. "Cool, right?"

"Sure, boss."

"How much did those clothes cost you?"

"Do we have to go through this again? Three hundred fifty for the shirt, which has UV protection; two seventy-five for the pants..."

Tom started laughing and then Nora joined him, and soon their exclamations of shock and disgust drowned out the rest of Randall's explanation. He was making it up anyway. He didn't remember what he paid for each individual piece of clothing. He never had, but he did enjoy pulling one over on his boss.

As much as she denied it, Randall understood that Nora was his boss. It might not look that way in the Agency's organizational chart. He understood that in one sense they were partners, equals even. But in another sense he was very aware that he still had a lot to learn from Nora Brooks. As long as that was the case, he planned on calling her his boss.

The September day was beautiful, with a predicted high of eighty-two, though they wouldn't stay to see that. They'd opted to hike out at daybreak. No one really wanted to sizzle in the sun at high noon. Randall had endured enough of that to last a lifetime.

He and Nora had flown into Grand Junction on the red eye and driven west for nearly two hours. Tom had the longer drive coming from Zion, five hours north, then east. Their plans were to hike for half a day, then take a behind-the-scenes tour of historic structures in the park, and finally end with an evening at a nearby resort.

Honestly, he couldn't believe Nora had agreed to the two days off, let alone suggested they both take them. She had insisted that it was all Tom's idea, and that they owed him.

Randall couldn't find any good reason to argue with that. As far as he was concerned, both Tom and Nora had saved his life. They'd somehow managed to climb back to his position after shooting Karvatsky's tablet. Tom had applied new clotting compresses to his arm and re-bandaged it. Instead of giving him Tylenol, Tom had offered the morphine tablets he carried in his medical pack, and Randall had readily accepted. He didn't remember a lot about the medical helicopter. When he'd woken twenty-four hours later in a Denver hospital, Nora and Tom had been sitting in the visitor chairs staring at him.

All that seemed like a distant memory on this beautiful fall day.

"Why'd you bring us out here, Tom?" Nora sounded more curious than irritated.

It was pretty obvious to Randall that she was enjoying the morning.

"Yeah, No offense..." Randall turned in a circle, once again taking in the spectacular vista. "The arches are...stunning, but I've probably seen enough red sandstone to last me a lifetime."

Tom pulled down on his mustache and offered them a slow smile. "I wanted you to experience the beauty of the place, to see what you saved and what it means to people."

An older couple strolled by hand-in-hand.

A group of tourists hammed it up for a selfie shot.

A man and woman with a baby stroller stopped to read the history of the arches.

Nora glanced at Randall and acted as if she was seriously considering what he'd said. "Now that we're not chasing a terrorist..."

"Or being shot at..."

"Or having to rappel while being chased by said terrorist..."

"And being shot at while rappelling."

"I guess I can see what you mean."

The day turned into one that Randall knew he would always remember. The memories of lying in the canyon, waiting for Nora to send help even as the blood continued to seep from his bandaged arm...those things had faded. It seemed to him that terror did that. Given time, it became something that you could look at and try to understand, but it lost its power over you.

And truthfully there were worse things to haunt him than that. What might have happened in Zion and San Francisco, Portland and Seattle. What had happened in Albuquerque and Phoenix and San Diego. Those images would take a bit longer to fade, especially given the national news coverage.

But looking back on what they'd experienced together, the actual moments ran together in a blur of danger and camaraderie and wonder that they'd all made it through unscathed.

Mostly unscathed. He'd always have a scar on his left arm, and it would be a while before he could lift the same amount of weight with it as he did with his right.

But he could lift his weapon.

He could do his job.

He was grateful for those things. As his pop was more than willing to point out, "Focus on gratitude, son." Good advice from a man who had never chased a terrorist, but still understood more about life than Randall probably ever would.

Which made him think there was a lot his parents and Nora had in common. He started laughing at that thought since his parents and Nora were about as opposite as people could be. His laughter caused Tom and Nora to turn and look at him as if he was possibly losing his grasp on things.

Instead of explaining, he waved toward Tom's National Park jeep. "Let's go see this behind-the-scenes tour."

§

It was only a fifty-seven mile drive to the resort where they were staying, but due to the winding roads it took almost two hours. Randall drove their rental, claiming it was the perfect opportunity to listen to his audiobook without being interrupted. "Go with Tom. You have the pleasure of my company every week."

"He's changed," Nora said as she buckled up in the passenger seat of Tom's jeep.

"How so?"

"More serious, somehow. Less arrogant."

"Almost dying will do that to a person."

"I suppose."

The drive to the resort took them out of Arches National Park and through the Castle Valley. Nora felt the tension in her unwind as she stared out at the natural beauty. Perhaps Tom was right. Maybe she needed to see what had been saved.

The resort itself was just over the Colorado border and unlike anywhere Nora had ever stayed before. Nestled in the midst of the red rock canyons, the resort itself probably rated higher than five stars—golf course, swimming pools, and of course exceptional dining choices.

Nora was glad she'd packed something other than black slacks and a button–up, neutral color top. The sky-blue dress she slipped into felt light, soft against her skin, and she had to admit it did accentuate her red hair.

She turned abruptly from the mirror.

Why was she thinking about how she looked in blue?

She was a top agent in the cyber division, not a star-struck teenager. Was she star struck?

Her feelings for Tom confused her. They'd talked or texted nightly since the events in Zion National Park. Those same events had forged a friendship that would have normally taken years to cultivate. She didn't know if what they had would go beyond friendship, but she did know that she was glad he was in her life.

Maybe it was her appetite, or perhaps it was the world-class chef who prepared their food, but dinner was the best she could remember.

"Randall's at home in this kind of establishment." She raised her wineglass to her partner, then took a sip of the smooth red cabernet.

"She only says that because I'm rich."

"How much did your outfit cost?"

"Not that again."

"You look good, Randall." Her voice softened, her mood suddenly less playful. "Really, you look good."

"Are you hitting on me?"

"I am not."

Tom sat back and folded his arms. "I've missed this—watching you two work together is both entertaining and enlightening."

Which served to ease the tightness in Nora's throat. The server brought three desserts, followed by the best cup of coffee Nora had ever drank.

"I could get used to this," she admitted. She glanced at Randall and cleared her throat, then directed her next statement toward Tom. "We spoke about it on the flight this morning, and if there are any...uh... questions that you have about recent events, then we'll be happy to try to answer."

"In other words, she received approval from the director," Randall explained.

"You did help us."

"If not for you, Nora and I might both be dead."

Tom sat back and studied them. Finally he said, "I think you might be overstating how much I helped, but sure. I have a few questions."

"Go for it." Nora sipped more of her coffee and wished the cup was bottomless.

Randall, who some days seemed to understand Nora better than she understood herself, caught the eye of the server, who hustled over with a refill.

"Was Karvatsky's device a nuclear one, like the others that exploded across the country?"

"It was." Nora smiled at the server and took another sip. It was decaf, but she still should probably slow down. Sleep was precious, and she didn't want to disturb hers by over indulging. "As Randall suspected, it was controlled by the tablet which is why it didn't detonate."

"The man I shot? The man with Karvatsky?"

"A cousin that he'd brought over on a work visa."

"Mario Morelli?"

Nora glanced at Randall, who took up the story. "Mario saw the light, it appears. No more solitary runs on closed park trails. Turns out that he has a graduate degree in advanced mathematics. He applied to the agency and was hired last week."

"Well. All good answers." Tom sat back, picked up his fork, then set it back down. "The overall attack included a dozen devices, and a dozen teams?"

Nora shook her head. "Fourteen, actually. Two were just over the Canadian side of the border."

"Only the Albuquerque, Phoenix, and San Diego attacks were successful. Due to the high altitude of the devices, casualties were minimal." Randall frowned at the table. "Too many, though. Still too many."

"I don't really understand that, and the news reports seem to be conflicting. What exactly did people die from if not from the nuclear detonation?"

"Some from the temporary lack of 9-1-1 service... heart attacks, strokes, even a few fires where the crews didn't reach the site in time." Randall finished his coffee and dessert, pushed the plate and cup away. "The fact that it took place in June hurt us. Some of the older citizens, with complicating medical conditions and no air conditioning...they didn't make it."

"All three affected metropolitan areas have replaced roughly sixty percent of their damaged infrastructure. They hope to be at one hundred percent in the next sixty days."

"But what we found was that the communities pulled together in ways that we couldn't have anticipated. The fatalities could have been much worse." Randall stretched his arms over his head and yawned. "Sorry. That flight we caught...it was super early."

"My partner needs his beauty sleep."

"I do, and on that, I'll say good night." He stood and shook hands with Tom. "If you ever need anything..."

"I have your number."

Randall placed his hand on Nora's shoulder. "Good night, boss."

"Good night, Randall."

Nora watched him walk away. She realized she'd just spent the evening with the two people in the world that she felt the most comfortable with. Glancing over at Tom, she couldn't have stopped the smile forming on her lips.

"This is nice. Thank you for inviting us."

"Care to take an evening stroll?"

"I would love that."

Although the resort was quite large, the lighting was night-sky friendly. They walked out on the patio, then down a trail that bordered the swimming pools.

Tom pointed to a sign that read *Overlook* and raised his eyebrows.

"Yes. Good idea."

Standing there, beneath the canopy of stars, Nora felt content for the first time in a very long while. She realized with a start that it was more than that. She felt happy, and not because she'd caught a cyber terrorist or stopped an attack. She felt happy because of who she was with, and the fact that she'd stopped struggling against so many things that were out of her control.

"You changed my life, you know."

"Did I, now?" Tom moved behind her, wrapped his arms around her waist, and waited. He was good at that, waiting for her to put difficult-to-explain things into words.

"I wasn't a very trusting person when I met you."

"Hazards of the job, I expect."

"I was completely on the fence about God and the fact that He could care about me, about us."

"And now?"

"I'm rethinking that. Or maybe I should say I'm re-feeling that. What conclusions I've drawn tend to come from my heart more than my head." She hesitated, then craned her head back, resting her head on Tom's shoulder and looking up at the stars. "Who can look at that and not believe someone created it?"

"I happen to agree with you."

She pivoted in his arms, tried to study his face in the darkness. "I don't want to be a fox-hole believer, but when I was hanging from that rope next to you, when I thought of how the pendant saved Randall...suddenly I did believe."

"Most everyone says a fox-hole prayer at some point in their life. I don't think God holds that against us."

She stood on tiptoe, kissed him on the lips.

He smiled, she could feel that more than see it, then tightened his arms around her and kissed her more thoroughly.

Hand in hand, they turned and headed back toward the resort.

"I could get used to being spoiled like this."

"I was hoping you'd say that."

"I'm not talking about the resort. I'm talking about you."

"And I was hoping that was what you meant."

They walked up the steps and into the lobby.

Nora had the sense that she was stepping into the next stage of her life. She didn't know what it would hold. She knew she would continue her job, keep working with Randall and trying to stop cyber attacks. It was in her blood, and she was good at it.

But now she understood that there was another part of her life as well. A part she was looking forward to exploring.

The End

༄

Author's Note

This book is dedicated to my friend, Carol Lilly, who led me on several death-defying hikes. I'm glad we survived!

My understanding is that nuclear EMP devices that could be carried in a backpack or suitcase do not currently exist. While there are dangers associated with high altitude nuclear explosions, the likelihood and extremity of such an attack has apparently been vastly over-emphasized in books and movies. I apologize for taking liberties with this scenario in my story, but it was too tempting to pass up.

I'll be the first to admit that my grasp of technological advances is less than complete; however, I am concerned about our growing dependence on technology both personally and globally. This series is designed to raise awareness regarding that dependence, as well as any corresponding vulnerability. If the subject interests you, I suggest you do some research. In my opinion, knowledge is a good thing.

As is always the case, I am grateful for my pre-readers, Kristy and Tracy. This story was also made better by Teresa, who served as editor, cover designer, and formatter. All three of you are awesome.

And finally ...always giving thanks to God the Father for everything, in the name of our Lord Jesus Christ (Ephesians 5:20).

Blessings,
Vannetta

§

About the Author

Vannetta Chapman writes inspirational fiction full of grace. She is a *PW* and *USA Today* bestselling author of over thirty novels in a variety of genres, including Amish romances, Amish mysteries, romantic suspense, and dystopian. Vannetta is also an ACFW Carol Award winner for best mystery of the year (2012). She currently resides in the Texas Hill Country.

For more information, visit her at
www.VannettaChapman.com.

Share your thoughts with Vannetta at
vannettachapman@gmail.com.

Read Vannetta's blog or sign up for her newsletter at
www.VannettaChapman.com.

໑

Also by Vannetta Chapman

The Remnant Series
Overshadowed * Deep Shadows
Raging Storm * Light of Dawn

Defenders of America Series
Coyote's Revenge * Roswell's Secret

Jacobs Family Series
Hidden * Protected

Agatha's Amish B&B Series
Dead Wrong

The Shipshewana Amish Mysteries
Falling to Pieces * A Perfect Square
Material Witness

The Amish Village Mysteries
Murder Simply Brewed * Murder Tightly Knit
Murder Freshly Baked

The Amish Bishop Mysteries
What the Bishop Saw
When the Bishop Needs an Alibi
Who the Bishop Knows

Find these and more at
vannettachapman.com/books/amish-mystery/.

Made in the USA
San Bernardino, CA
13 May 2020

71725816R00188